ALICE
WONDERLAND

SEX IN
WONDERLAND

WRITTEN BY

LISA HARRY

CONTENTS

CHAPTER 01

DOWN THE RABBIT HOLE

Chapter summary: *A 25 year girl called Alice is minding her own business until she encounters a certain White Rabbit.*

It was a sunny spring day and out in a large flowery meadow just outside the city of Edinburgh, there was a young woman of about 25 years of age was walking through and feeling annoyed with life. The girl's name was Alice Kingsley and wore tight navy-blue jeans, a white blouse with a dark blue camisole over it, black walking boots and a choke collar. Though she might have not thought of it, she was a very beautiful young lady with blue eyes and long blonde hair that at first had all the featured that any red blooded male would have wanted in a girl; sadly most people didn't seem to notice this about her. Instead, it was her large ass.

For as far back as she could remember, everyone had made fun of her large rear end with one unfortunate chapter of her life during High School was that of the girls making horrid jokes about her and most of the boys attempting to spank her whenever she walked by. She really could not understand why she had been cursed with such an enormous bottom, but even if she was to ignore that, that wasn't the end of her troubles.

Alice never had any real friends, and this was always about her absent minded personality and curious nature which often got her into trouble such as never paying attention in class ("What is point of reading a book without any pictures in it?" She had asked her English teacher once) to what others said and this was partly the reason why she had been never successful in having a relationship (most only ever wanting to grope her ass not surprisingly) or having a stable job.

Bottom line (no pun intended), she was totally out of place here and Alice had grown to feel this world was too boring for her.

"Oh, to find a world of my own," Alice sighed as she sat down at the base of a large oak tree. "They say I speak just nonsense, what do they know?"

'They' being her parents, perhaps the ones that caused much annoyance in her life. Alice came from an upper middle-class background in which her mother and father had wanted her to drop her childish ways and act more like a lady, though Alice despite her parent's best attempts at making her think one way such as sending her to a private school to achieve a high education, their efforts had failed as not only was she something of a socially awkward person to many but deep down had

something of a frisky side that was waiting to come out.

Her relationship with her parents had gotten more strained as she became an adult to the point in which once she had moved out, she never spoke to them again though the blonde haired girl suspected her parents were glad she was out of their lives.

As she began threading a daisy chain together from a patch of flowers, she was sitting next to; more of her typical childish behaviour on display. It was then as she finished making the chain, she suddenly had an idea about nonsense she said earlier.

"That's it! If I had a world of my own, everything would be full of nonsense and I wouldn't have to act like a lady. But where would I find such a place?"

She looked around at the vast meadow before her and pondered the situation. She had always liked coming over to this location many times to escape and just be herself which given the fact she lived in a small flat on her own with nosy neighbours around wondering what she was doing which was pretty much everyday.

The sun was blazing down with hardly any clouds in the sky, and Alice was glad she'd found this tree to take shelter under as she could keep cool while she looked over the rolling hills of insects buzzing around and distract road traffic could be heard heading to and from the city.

Looking around making sure no one was around, she found herself getting hot and bothered by the sun and it wasn't long before she found it hard to control her urges, so she slipped her hand down her jeans and began to pleasure herself.

Oh yes, it was certainly not how lady should act according to her mother, but Alice was a girl like many who had urges who needed to let it out and out here was always a perfect place for her to have her private time.

Alice moaned with pleasure as she fingered herself, she wished though she could find someone who could not only give her such pleasure but also like her for who she was as a person. Sadly, all the men in her life only cared to either spank or stare at her butt and how she was told to act like a lady according to her stuck up parents.

Oh, what a life for poor Alice!

She didn't know how long she had been doing it for but she didn't care as she ended her world of pleasure and thrills with a moaning climax and wet underwear. Such was it fun to act all naughty like that. She finally rested her back on the side of the tree and gazed at the world around her.

Little did she know then was that soon at that moment, her life would change forever.

"Nothing really changes here," Alice said to herself. "Just the usual wildlife such as birds, bugs, a rabbit in a waistcoat-"

She made a double take thinking the sun had got to her, but her eyes widened in shock at the incredulous sight running along the dirt path some few meters away. There was indeed a white rabbit with a grey, yellow waistcoat, grey trousers, a red jacket while holding a large pocket watch. The rabbit's clothes were very Victorian looking from what Alice could make out and now her mind was going mad about who or where this rabbit was from.

Even where sat, Alice could see this rabbit was the biggest she had seen, about roughly half her size and looked totally out of place here, but that was not the only thing that would stun Alice next. The rabbit looked at the watch and gasped in horror.

"My goodness I'm late! Whatever shall I do?" It suddenly spoke up with a feeble and worried male voice and hurried along the path bemoaning about his luck and timing.

For Alice, not only was she left stunned at what she had just witnessed a talking rabbit, but her curiosity was well and truly sparked and whenever that happened, she was left in her own world. Good luck trying to get her out of that.

"Oh, Mr. Rabbit! Please wait!" She cried out as she stood up and began running after the rabbit who was well in front of her, though she didn't know why she found the urge to call this strange rabbit as 'Mr Rabbit'.

The white rabbit had then gone off the path and was heading to a small woodland on the edge of the meadow which had quite thick grass growing, which was q uite hard for Alice to walk through even though she had her sturdy walking boots on to help her get through.

She was fortunate to get there as soon as she did was

that by the time she got there, she only managed to catch sight of the white rabbit scuttling into a rabbit hole under a set of bushes and into the darkness.

As Alice tilted her head at the hole in the ground, it dawned on her that this wasn't just any ordering rabbit hole, but rather a large rabbit hole it was. One that was large enough to fit not only a giant rabbit, but maybe a person...?

The blonde-haired girl suddenly felt a sense of excitement about what she might find in that hole, so taken as a matter of fact that any thoughts about how she might have if she was to get out of the hole were forgotten about.

Curiosity always was her worst enemy.

"I wonder why he was in such a hurry?" Alice pondered, "it must be a party he's going to...but an awfully curious place to have a party. Oh, silly me!

Rabbits live underground so of course that's where he'll go!"

She finished her rambling and got on her hands and knees and began to crawl into the rabbit hole. Peering into the hole in which she could get a better look, she was amazed to see how the tunnel inside seemed to go down a steep gradient and wondered what was inside this hole. She might not have had the best knowledge about tunnelling but even she seemed suspicious about that something wasn't right here...

She managed to get half her body into the hole but found difficulty with the lower half of her body. Oh yes, her blasted bottom had gotten her into q uite literally a tight spot to which she moaned and groaned trying to wriggle her way through into the hole. She only hoped no one was outside as she knew it would be embarrassing for her as rather than rescue her, they use the chance to ogle or spank her rear on display.

It was not helped that whenever she did get her bottom stuck like this with her moaning it would get her rather flustered and oddly would turn her on. Such were her urges she always seemed to have at the worst possible moment.

After some more wriggling and a small pray hoping no one would notice her, she finally dragged her whole body into the hole and began crawling further into the tunnel. Part of her should've been thinking about how she was going to get out given how hard it was to get into the hole in the first place, but she had gotten so far by this point that there was no turning back.

Curiously, the further she got in and even with the fading sunlight on the outside making it hard to find her way forward the deeper she went in, she could see that the tunnel was getting not only wider but more to the point in which she could almost stand.

However, her absence mind and lack of vision in the dark would q uite literally prove to be her downfall and with one final crawl, her left hand suddenly felt the ground disappear and so sudden this was that she didn't have enough time to react as before then, her whole body fell forward down what turned out to Alice's horror a large black hole heading straight down towards the centre of the earth and surely no way back for Alice.

She screamed on the way down, tumbling forwards in the dark which was becoming more apparent the deeper she was falling and not knowing what was happening and quite rightly thought that this was her end.

This was in fact only the start of an adventure in a new world that would be beyond her wildest imagination.

Alice couldn't really comprehend what was happening as she was plummeting to her doom, though if she did, she couldn't make it up, even for her wild imagination. Only this morning she had left the rich but rather boring surroundings of her native Marchmont district in Edinburgh to relax in a field on her own until she saw a large white rabbit, following it towards a rabbit hole in the ground in which she only managed to get through thanks to that blasted bottom she had before now falling to what was clearly a bottomless pit towards what seemed to be her doom.

What a way for the curious and foolish Alice to end her life, a bizarre situation that one couldn't make it up. As she fell further tumbling down the rabbit hole her screaming gradually began to stop and instead it began to dawn on her at just not only at just how deep this hole was but for some reason she seemed to be slowing down. The good news was her tumbling had stopped with her now facing the right way up she began take in that something wasn't quite right as her falling was now a gentle descent.

Alice looked down past her feet at the endless darkness, her heart hammering again her chest over the insane situation that had happened and she peered down into the darkness below her with her slender legs wide open which Alice suspected might have something to do with slower her down.

"Well!" Alice said to herself in amazing. "After such a fall as this, I shall think nothing of tumbling down stairs again! How brave they'll all think of me at home!"

Home. It then only then Alice thought about how was she suppose to get out of here the deeper she was going. With Alice inside the hole and very unlikely not able to get out for a while, what would others think about her sudden absence? Then again as soon as that thought filtered through her, her mind drifted off thinking about something else.

"This is all very curious," Alice muttered, her voice echoing in the darkness. "What on Earth is down here?"

Her rambling stopped when suddenly out of the darkness she could see a faint light below her and as she narrowed her eyes to adjust to the darkness, she then realised that it was a gas lamp of some sort. As she slowly fell further down the hole, she found a switch just barely in the darkness and passing slowly by she used this chance to flick the switch to try and make the place brighter at least.

She managed flicked the switch as she slowly drifted past and the rabbit hole was engulfed in a warm yellowish glow and Alice was finding this more curious by the minute. The walls of the

rabbit hole were lined not of dirt or earth, but rather

what seemed to be a patterned green wall which had many crooked looking portrait frames all over the wall. It all got more stranger as the light she had turned on was now slowly changing its colour to glows of green, purple, red and blue in random order and that wasn't including the fact that around her were bits of house furniture such as tables, chairs, desks, clocks and very distinctively ancient looking furniture she might've only seen once on that rather dull day out at Hopetoun House with her parents, not only was that another story but this experience was truly fascinating for Alice as she past a mirror of her reflection that to her amazement was instead of going down like her was instead going up!

If all this was just unexplainable, Alice began to feel rather relaxed about all this. She didn't know how long she had been falling for, a minute? An hour? A day even? Time just felt like it was stopping the deeper she went with her gaze on a grandfather clock on the side of the wall that had the time slowly turning as if it's gears were about to break. She could not for the life of her know just what was going on and with that also came on how she was starting to feel. It was also starting to get warmer though she couldn't tell if something strange was causing it or it was just her.

"Oh my goodness," Alice purred in weird enjoyment. "How on earth am I feeling so...excited?"

She couldn't understand why, but the whole slow journey down to wherever it was leading her was making her feel rather aroused at the weird thrill of it all.

"Bloody hell, why is this making me feel so good?" Alice moaned as she began rubbing her crotch with desire.

While many would've been scared for their lives in this situation, only Alice could find sexual pleasure falling down a rabbit hole.

During that moment, the blonde-haired woman's bright blue eyes widened as there on the wall was a large portrait of two people but one of them looked a lot like her! Alice was lost for words as she drifted past it as the two people in the portrait were dressed in what looked like royal attire with the blonde woman had her hair tied in a bun and wore a form fitting blue dress while beside her was a handsome looking brunette man dressed in a red suit and a rather strange matching red top hat.

What was the most apparent thing for Alice that the couple in the portrait looked very happy, like a blessed couple...

So taken by this that she almost didn't notice that the walls were starting to close in until what felt like the last moment. Perhaps it was a sign her fall was nearing its end! Alice looked down and she saw that the hole was narrowing, like the thin neck of a bottle. She grew increasingly worried, concerned over what would happen in that small tube-like part of this deep hole with her legs wide open.

Perhaps this was the halfway mark, and thus meant that her journey was nearing its end? That was all well and good, but she needed to think q uickly about how she would get through the narrow part which was coming up on her fast. She conjured an idea q uick enough, just as the narrow part was rising beneath her. Just as the walls contacted her black shoes, she closed her legs together so she would fit her whole body through the narrow part of the hole and hoped that her certain rear end wouldn't cause any problems.

It did though. Her fall came to a shuddering stop her her hips firmly stuck.

"Oh, this blasted bottom!" She groaned as she

eventually freed herself after much wriggling and flaring of her legs trying to get out.

Turns out that maybe being stuck was not quite such a bad idea. She fell through like a rock through the narrow part as she disappeared into the narrow bottleneck. Alice released a shrill scream as she looked up and saw the first half of her journey quickly fall further and further away from her.

The farther she fell, the more the rabbit hole felt like a death trap than the leisurely float it had been only minutes before. How long could the narrow part of a hole be? Alice soon realized that the hole she had been travelling down was shaped like an hourglass, and she was travelling through the narrow part that connected the two larger halves. Maybe time had frozen outside the hole since she had fallen such as how slow the clock had been going round? It might have been possible though it still concerned her how long she had been gone, falling (albeit rather leisurely) through here. Her plummet was now a fast one, as she had brought her legs together and had formed something of a human rocket, and she could hear nothing except the wind whipping at her jeans and only fear possessed her as she wondered whether this was the end of her as she continued down. Down, down, down.

The narrow part continued on a ways, until her lungs had long lost air for her to form screams. Was this how the rest of her fall would pan out?! Surely it can't! She'd die instantly if she hit the bottom now! If she was to survive, the hole had to widen soon and hope for a miracle.

Finally, the bottleneck widened and bloomed out into the shame of a dome, meaning it was safe for her to open her legs and return to her leisurely drift. Alice didn't waste anytime to widen her legs like she had done prior to the bottle neck and thankfully everything slowed down again though it did jolt poor

Alice upright. The fall immediately slowed, much to her relief.

"Goodness me!" Alice gasped clasping her hand over her beating heart. "How long does the hole go on for?

What she didn't know then was that thin tube was in fact a wormhole that connected Alice's world to this strange new place that not only felt warmer down here like a spring day before she entered the rabbit hole, but smelt like fresh flowers. Alice couldn't see any flowers around her, though she did see on one of the walls a map hanging up of some strange looking map that on the bottom spelt the words 'Wonderland' in red capital letters.

Alice had to smile at the name as she thought about it. "Well, this 'Wonderland' so far is already living up to its name, though...what if I should fall straight through the earth, and come out the other side where people walk upside down?"

She laughed at her own q uestion.

"Oh, but that's silly. Nobody walks that way!"

The rabbit hole was starting to look more and more like a normal home the deeper she went such as the dirt walls giving way to ornate wallpaper with fleur-de-lis patterns, funny thing was that if she was falling endless then she wouldn't mind living in such comfy looking surroundings. Alice wondered to herself how long she had been falling, and just how much longer she would have to fall.

Her wish would come sooner than expected when lot a second later after saying it, she had finally reached the bottom of the rabbit hole and her bottom had come into contact with a red leather couch; such a curious thing to use to stop a long fall. As she stood up, she saw the room was what could be best described as some crazy art project with the title floor of black and white making a curious pattern as well as the walls being a mix of patterned wooden panels and brick face. The corridor she realised she was in had no straight lines in it and the room felt like it was bending to

the side no matter where she looked.

Alice then glanced up at where she came from and saw how small the hole looked from down here and wondered how one was to get back out again. But this thought was forgotten about when at the other end of the corridor, she caught sight of the certain white rabbit she'd followed all the way down here and immediately began chasing him.

"Oh Mr Rabbit, please!" Alice called out to the white rabbit as she could hear the rabbit worrying about being late.

She followed the rabbit down a weird looking

corridor in which she had time to process her surroundings. It was all mad looking with the walls either closing in or spreading apart and were nothing like anything she had seen where she had come from; Alice felt something click in her in that moment in which something about this place seemed right up her street.

She then found herself at a crossroads where three more corridors went to different locations and she couldn't find the white rabbit anywhere. Then to her left she heard the sound of a door creaking shut and Alice knew right away that this had to be where that rabbit had got to.

She rushed over to the door and opened it...only to find another smaller door behind it. To her frustration, she ended up having to open five doors that not only eventually showed the way forward, but the opening was so small that the only way to get through was to crawl. If that wasn't weird enough, her fat ass for once did not get stuck as there was just enough room to get through.

"How curious," Alice said to herself at that situation before looking around at the new room she had crawled into. "Curiouser and Curiouser..."

It was indeed curious. Alice found himself in a large box room featuring four different coloured walls of red, purple, green and blue as well as a tiled marble floor pattern.

"Well...I'm certainly not in Marchmont anymore," Alice muttered to herself. Then on the other end of the room, she saw another door closing and a set of red curtains covering it up. No prizes as to guess where that rabbit had gone now and she hurried along to the other side of the room where she passed by a small glass table in which she didn't take much notice of as she focused on following the white rabbit.

She hadn't realised how small the curtains were from the distance as when she got there and got on her knees, she opened the curtains revealing a green door about two feet tall and maybe just enough for her to crawl through. She grabbed the golden doorknob when suddenly it groaned as she tried turning the knob. The doorknob was alive! Shocked, Alice gasped falling on her backside. "I beg your pardon, sir!"

"Ugh, no it's q uite alright," the doorknob replied before looking at her again. With those clothes she certainly wasn't from around here. "I say, who are you and where are you from?"

"Well, my name is Alice Kingsley and I'm from Edinburgh...have you heard of it?" the blonde- haired girl asked while finding it strange she was talking to what should've been an none living object.

The door knob rolled it's eyes. "Never heard of the place, say, you are a human from Earth are you not?"

"Well...yes, this is Earth, right?"

The doorknob chuckled. "Oh no dear girl, this is Wonderland. Anyway, how did you get here anyway?"

Alice was wide eyed. Was she was on some other world? Certainly not Edinburgh that was for sure or God forbid maybe Glasgow (then again that city was an entirely different world to Edinburgh). She had many q uestions to ask but then she remembered why she was here in the first place.

"Well, I was looking for a white rabbit...have you seen him?"

"Oh, him? Of course," the doorknob replied and opened his mouth/keyhole that was large another for Alice to slip her hand through. Peering through it, she could just make out seeing that certain rabbit rushing into a woodland outside the door.

Alice beamed. "There he is! I simply must go through!"

The doorknob thought otherwise. "Sorry, you're simply much too big to get through." "But how can I?"
"Look by that table," the doorknob instructed. "You'll find a key and bottle to get you through."

At this point, Alice should've been listening but that had never been her strength as a wonderful smell got her attention. On the table along with the key and bottle of liq uid that had the words 'Drink Me' on a label, there was a third object that made Alice hungry with desire. A small piece of cake.

Ever since she was young, Alice had always loved cake in which she would've happily lived a life on eaten just cake and any advice she had to listen to went out of the window as she stared hungrily at the lemon slice cube that had the words 'Eat Me' on it.

"Don't mind if I do," Alice giggled and went for it. The doorknob was horrified. "No, Alice! Don't do it!"
But it was too late, Alice very un-lady like eaten the cube of cake and moaned with pleasure as she felt it go down...then she suddenly found herself growing until she found herself standing at over twenty feet tall, thankfully her clothes hadn't ripped but seemed to have stretched along with her.

"What has happened to me?!" Alice cried out at her predicament.

"You foolish girl!" The doorknob scolded. "You were only to drink the bottle to shrink and get the key!"

In her flustered state, she bent down as best she could to grab the small bottle in her large hands to gulp down what was in the bottle. Then as suddenly as she had grown, she was shrinking at a rapid rate until she was now just two feet tall and the right size to get through the door.

"Finally! Now you can let me through," Alice grinned but the doorknob was looking evermore annoyed with the blonde girl.

"Oh, for heavens sake you stupid woman...you left the key up on the table!"

Alice gasped at her foolishness of only now spotting the key high up on the table. "Oh dear! What shall I do to get out?"

She placed her hands on her hips looking up and thinking what she could do while only the doorknob was starting to find this Alice girl rather tasty, especially that large bottom on her that

seemed to have the words 'eat me' on them like on

the cake. He then had an idea and Alice would soon find out that no matter what world she was in, her ass was always going to cause her trouble.

The doorknob opened his keyhole wide open and began to suck the air through it with such strength that Alice began to feel being dragged backwards off her feet.

"Whatever are you Oh!" Alice began to ask before she found herself flying headfirst towards the keyhole and quickly found herself with the upper half of her body on the other side and her lower half trapped. Once again her bottom had got her stuck again.

The doorknob was not expecting Alice's ass to be that big and could be heard struggling to try and swallow her. Alice began wriggling and kicking her legs furiously trying to get out, yet being trapped (again) was getting her horny and the worst possible time.

"You pervert!" Alice cried in anger. "That's a whole new meaning to the term 'nob head!' But goodness I have to stop feeling so...wait...oh no, not now!"

Just then, she could feel a gurgling in her stomach thanks to the drink and cake she had which was coming together and about to come out in the only way possible.

She let out a fart.

Alice was utterly mortified at letting off wind like that, but for some reason if it was either her struggling or letting one rip, she managed to get herself out of the keyhole and tumbled onto other side and she could hear the doorknob moaning on the other side was moaning about the smell that Alice had caused. But she had no regrets and for good reason.

"Serves you right!" She called out angrily.

She got back on her feet looking on the other side of the door seeing that there were no walls by it and it was just there on it's own. Turning round, Alice gasped at the view before her, a beautiful and brightly coloured woodland with strange looking trees, giant mushrooms and a warm breeze in the air that made her feel strangely right at home. It was a sort of world she wanted to find and now her dream place was here.

Without further thought, she headed forward into the unknown as Alice began her adventures in this strange new world called Wonderland.

CHAPTER 02
WONDERLAND

Chapter Summary: Alice soon makes her first steps in Wonderland and meets some of the crazy inhabitants...

Wonderland. To say Alice had never seen such a truly fascinating place was really saying a lot. She went along a reddish dirt path heading into the woods and was truly captivated by her new and wondrous surroundings.

Everything just seemed to be vibrant and alive like all out a cartoon from the likes of the colours on the trees, grass, flowers and even the sunny blue sky, which had a tiny hint of purple in it, seemed clearer and more open in a way. Though considering the dull, lifeless, and mostly cloudy surroundings of Edinburgh of where she came from before, it wasn't much to top that.

Either way, Alice felt something inside of her saying

that this place was for her and even then wonder if she would ever want to even return where she last came from.

She was amazed at seeing the large mushrooms that towered over her, seeing different colours of leaves such as blue and purple and wonder what strange creatures she might encounter next, after all if that strange white rabbit was anything to go by then who knows what lay in store for her. At that moment of thinking about the rabbit, she stopped in her tracks when she remembered as the whole reason she had ended up down here was to look for that rabbit and now with her in the middle of this forest with no sign of the white rabbit and most to her own annoyance no idea where to go next.

"Bother, now what do I do now?" Alice pouted placing her hands on her hips and trying to rationalise what to do next. All she could do however was look up at either the tall mushrooms and strange coloured trees and pondered if she should carry on looking or go somewhere different; who knew what this strange by fascinating world had in store for her.

Her thoughts were interrupted when she heard voices coming from her left and curious about who and where they were coming from, she went off the path towards a clearing through the bushes; maybe there was that white rabbit?

Alice soon found out that she was on a beach and the ocean was not blue, but purple. The beach wasn't sandy yellow, but sandy orange and the voices were coming from a party of animals all soaking wet, presumably having swam in the purple ocean.

They were indeed a strange looking party that assembled on the beach; the birds with draggled feathers, the animals with their fur clinging close to them, and all them dripping wet, cross, and uncomfortable. Alice had no idea just what they just done or what she had gotten herself into but she was curious to witness this meeting. She thought she could take a moment from chasing the white rabbit or maybe they knew where he might've gone.

The question of the meeting was of course of how to get dry again: the animals had a consultation about this, and after a few minutes of debating it had all seemed q uite natural to Alice as if there was nothing strange about it other than the fact they were large talking animals about her size.

Indeed, she was especially taken by a large well dressed Dodo that was having quite a long argument with a Loriini, who at last turned sulky, and would only say, "I am older than you, and must know better"; and this Alice would not allow without knowing how old it was, and, as the Loriini positively refused to tell its age, there was no more to be said.

Then the Dodo, who seemed to be a person of authority among them from what Alice could see was the leader, called out, "Sit down, all of you, and listen to me! I'll soon make you dry enough!"

They all sat down at once, in a large ring, with Alice now approaching the group to introduce herself. She was about to clear her throat to get their attention when the Dodo started to speak.

"Now then, are you all ready? This is the driest thing I know. Silence all round if you please! 'William the Conq ueror, whose cause was favoured by the pope, was soon submitted to by the English, who wanted leaders, and had been of late much accustomed to usurpation and conquest. Edwin and Morcar, the earls of Mercia and Northumbria—'"

"Ugh!" groaned the Mouse, with a shiver. Alice smiled hearing a bit of history she did vaguely know about in High School, though vaguely as her mind always wandered. Though around her it seemed not many appreciated hearing it.

"I beg your pardon?!" asked the Dodo, frowning, but very politely: "Did you speak?" "Hurry up!" cried the Mouse hastily.

"I thought you did," grumbled the Dodo. `-I proceed. "'Edwin and Morcar, the earls of Mercia and Northumbria, declared for him: and even Stigand, the patriotic archbishop of Canterbury, found it advisable-'"

"Found what?" asked the Duck.

"Found it," the Dodo replied rather crossly: "of course you know what 'it' means."

"I know what 'it' means well enough, when I find a thing," said the Duck: "it's generally a frog or a worm. The q uestion is, what did the archbishop find?"

The Dodo did not notice this q uestion and Alice was baffled how this whole conversation had nothing to do with how to dry but ancient history...history from her world. The Dodo nonetheless hurriedly went on, "'-found it advisable to go with Edgar Atheling to meet William and offer him the crown. William's conduct at first was moderate. But the insolence of his Normans—oh!"

The well-dressed Dodo had now noticed Alice standing there, who had been listening in to their meeting. "I say, you there!"

All the animals in the circle turned to gaze upon the human in the midst, not knowing what to make of this strange girl and her clothes of jeans and blue camisole that were not clearly of this world of Wonderland.

Alice began to greet herself, "Well then, terribly sorry to introduce myself but my name is—" "Are you wet my dear?" The Dodo interrupted her.
"I...pardon me?!"

"Are you wet strange human?"

"Well, suppose in more ways than one," Alice muttered q uietly with a hint of embarrassment. She wasn't exactly wrong considering of how she had soaked her own underwear since the start of this adventure while falling down the Rabbit Hole. She really couldn't control her urges.

They didn't get the double meaning of Alice's words and he solemnly rose to his feet to speak. "In that case...I move that the meeting adjourn, for the immediate adoption of more energetic remedies —"

"Speak English!" said the Eaglet. "I don't know the meaning of half those long words, and, what's more, I don't believe you do either!"

The Eaglet bent down its head to hide a smile: some

of the other birds tittered audibly.

"What I was going to say," said the Dodo in an offended tone, "was, that the best thing to get us dry would be a Caucus-race."

"What is a Caucus-race?" Asked Alice; not that she wanted much to know, but the Dodo had paused as if it thought that somebody ought to speak, and no one else seemed inclined to say anything.

"Why," said the Dodo, "the best way to explain it is to do it." (And, as you might like to try the thing yourself, some winter day, I will tell you how the dodo managed it.)

First it marked out a racecourse, in a sort of circle, (`the exact shape does not matter,' it said,) and then all the party were placed along the course, here and there. There was no `One, two, three, and away,' but they began running when they liked, and left off when they liked, so that it was not easy to know when the race was over.

Alice somehow found herself getting involved in this so-called race and after five minutes of this she was getting fed up. She had only wanted to know if any of them had seen the white rabbit and yet neither of them had even brought up any white rabbit nor had that they seemed willing to help her. Just as she was about to give up, she then looked up towards the woods running along the path was and caught a glance at who she had been looking for. The White Rabbit!

Where on earth he had gotten to in all this was strange, but then again Alice was starting to feel that logic and rational thinking never applied to this place after what she had experienced so far. She was just glad to see that she hadn't lost the white rabbit after all and maybe find out what he was out to do.

"Mr Rabbit!" Alice cried out and quickly ran after him while leaving the group of animals to carry on with the race they seemed determined to try and finish it (neither of them though caring about her sudden departure.)

So thus, Alice left the beach and headed back into the vibrant wood to find the white rabbit and maybe find something interesting and curious about Wonderland. Little did she know that her adventure in this strange world had only just started.

As she walked on, Alice simply lost track as to where she was going nor as to what time it was. Looking up through the tops of trees where she could see part of the sky, it seemed as the sky was turning a darker shade of purple as if to say evening was rolling in.

The frisky girl was beginning to realise that with how vast this woodland was, her hopes to try and find the white rabbit were now looking increasingly hopeless and that she had gone on a wild

goose chase for nothing while finding herself lost in this strange world that was most certainly not Earth. She couldn't q uite believe how long she had been out in this forest for and that if time was the same back on Earth then surely it would be getting close to the evening.

With the sense that she felt she had been on nothing sort of a wild goose chase, Alice huffed crossly and sat down on a fallen tree. "Oh, damn. Why did I follow that rabbit? Now I'll have to go back...that is, if I can find my way home...home."

Now Alice found herself in an unfortunate situation that she didn't know, other than perhaps asking the White Rabbit as to how to get to her world. Then again when she muttered the word 'home' it did not feel right as she never fit into anything, the oddest girl growing up in Scotland was she?

Truth be told she was feeling conflicted on her current predicament and where she truly belonged.

Checking her pockets, she found out that she had left her phone back up at her flat and there was no way to contact anyone, then again Alice scoffed at the notion of trying to get a signal out in this strange world if she had phone on her. Alice thought about her situation that even if she did know of a way back, would she want to go back to her dull and boring life?

She couldn't tell but the more she sat here and stared around at the strange yet oddly calm setting, the more she felt a feeling of excitement and wonder that all seem to be telling her that this was the place for her. Maybe she was stuck here forever but would anyone care for her?

Just that thought of being trapped on a strange world with no way back home was beginning to strangely turn her on (she always did have weird urges and fetishes) and she found herself slipping her two fingers under her jeans and started playing with herself for not the first time that day. She always needed to pleasure herself at the most inappropriate moments and places.

As she was in the process of getting her underwear wet once again, she had not noticed that up on a thick branch looking down at this horny girl was a strange creature with glowing yellow eyes and one large toothy grin.

Oh yes, she would be perfect it thought. Just as Alice was about to climax, she heard a voice from the trees singing and the girl gasped and stood up q uickly looking wide eyed.

"Who's there?!"

"T'was brilling and the slithy toves," sang a strange voice in which Alice saw the grin and big eyes. Alice didn't know what to think when she saw those mad yellow eyes, still his singing seemed nice she suppose.

"Now who could-"

"I be?" The voice interrupted and soon the thing in the trees revealed itself showing to be a large, chunky cat...a purple cat with pink stripes running along its body as well as a big fluffy tail. Truly unlike any cat that Alice had seen before.

"Why...you're a cat!" Alice smiled, forgetting that she had been caught doing something that the cat wasn't meant to see.

"A Cheshire Cat," the Cat replied using his fluffy tail to lift off his ears as if they were on a headband. The Cat only grinned when it saw Alice looking awestruck.

It looked good-natured, she thought. Still, the cat had

very long claws and a great many teeth, so she felt that it ought to be treated with respect. "Cheshire Puss," she began, rather timidly, as she did not at all know whether it would like the name: however, it only grinned a little wider. "Would you

tell me, please, which way I ought to go from here?"

"That depends a good deal on where you want to get to," said the Cat. "I don't much care where" said Alice. "Then it doesn't matter which way you go," said the Cat.

"-so long as I get somewhere," Alice added as an explanation.

"Oh, you're sure to do that," said the Cat, "if you only walk long enough."

Alice felt that this could not be denied, so she tried another question. "What sort of people live about here?"

"In that direction," the Cat said, waving its right paw round, `lives a Hatter: and in that direction,' waving the other paw, `lives a March Hare. Visit either you like: they're both mad, though I would say the Hatter might be right for you."

"But I don't want to go among mad people," Alice remarked with annoyance.

"Oh, you can't help that," said the Cat: "we're all mad here. I'm mad and surely soon you'll be mad."

"How do you know that I would be mad?" Asked Alice, though she was curious as to why the Cat was leaning on her to visit this Hatter.

"You must be," said the Cat, "or you wouldn't have come here."

Truth be told, the Cat did have a point. She was rather mad to go down that rabbit hole, get lost and start playing with herself in a strange woodland; all of this would have been avoided has she not decided to follow that rabbit. Her mother would have a fit if she could see what Alice was doing, but the blonde-haired woman didn't care for that; she just had mad urges... Alice didn't think that proved it at all; however, she went on.

"And how do you know that you're mad?"

"To begin with," said the Cat, "a dog's not mad. You grant that?" "I suppose so," replied Alice thoughtfully.
"Well, then," the Cat went on, "you see, a dog growls when it's angry, and wags its tail when it's pleased. Now I growl when I'm pleased, then I wag my tail when I'm angry. Therefore, I'm mad."

"I call it purring, not growling," Alice corrected.

"Call it what you like," replied the Cat. "But I can see you wish to know about the Mad Hatter?" "Well, of course," Alice nodded, "who is the Hatter?"

The Cat giggled and began to float down beside Alice to slowly start circling her. "He is like you Earth girl but not... a different species to you that I must add he is a lost king."

"A king? Alice spluttered at this unexpected fact. "But does he have a castle or a kingdom?"

"Oh, his family did once," the Cat reflected, "until the mad q ueen beheaded his family and left him

as the last of the Hightop clan... drove the Hatter all a bit mad. Since then, Wonderland has been ruled by the Queen of Hearts and always seems to be off her head in more ways than one."

Alice was now greatly intrigued but this revelation

about Wonderland. Kings, q ueens, and clans? Now her curiosity spark had been lit and this did not go unnoticed by the Cat.

The girl crossed her arms and muttered, "Goodness, he must feel lonely and"

"You'll be his perfect mate to help regain Wonderland," the Cat butted in and started giggling to himself as he floated back up to the branch he had been relaxing on before. It took a moment for Alice to dawn on her by what the Cat was suggesting to her and not surprisingly, she looked annoyed by such a scenario. "Well, I never! I would have to be mad to do a thing like that! I don't even know the man!"

"Oh, but you are mad already by the way you were playing with yourself just now," the Cat laughed. "Then again as I have already mentioned, we are all mad here for about the millionth time!"

Alice tried to respond to the Cat. Was she already slipping into madness the more time she spent here in Wonderland? While, she had no intention at following the Cat's proposal, she was curious to see who this so called 'Mad Hatter' was and if he was really all what the Cat was making him out to be.

So many thoughts came to Alice and this Hatter who was some lost king and an evil q ueen who now ruled Wonderland. Something in her curious nature made her want to know more about this strange land as she felt that with what the Cheshire Cat had told her that he had barely scratched the surface of what Wonderland had to offer. Before she could q uestion the Cat for any further details, she could see that the Cat was gone and nowhere around the area.

"Oh, well then," Alice sighed, "I suppose I need to find a place to rest, it is getting late and what is the time? Bother, I should've had a watch with me."

With that said, Alice began walking off in the direction in which the Cat had pointed and went off to find the Mad Hatter. Little was she to know that she was about to meet a man who was unlike anyone she had met before. Maybe then once she met him she was about to fall into more madness...with hopefully some tea and cake included. She really could do with some of the latter as her stomach began to gurgle.

CHAPTER 03
TWEEDLEDEE AND TWEEDLEDUM

Chapter Summary: *As Alice leaves the Cat, she encounters two more of the crazy world of Wonderland which she wonders if she loses part of her IQ listening to them...*

Although Alice was grateful for getting some direction from the Cat, she still felt annoyed at herself for wasting time back there with the Dodo and the other creatures taking part in their strange game which she wondered if they were still playing and oblivious to her departure.

"What nonsense," she huffed to herself, "can't believe I wasted time taking part in whatever it was they were trying to do!"

Still, there was the white rabbit to follow and that was her main goal and what should've been her only goal, then again there was the story about the Mad Hatter she had been told about...

The long blonde-haired girl took note of the weird colours the woods were with the bark on the trees being of teal, leaves being red like autumn leaves and the grass a mix of yellow, green, and brown. What a curious world this was for Alice and she found herself liking the place more and more which did make her think that once she found both the White Rabbit and maybe the Mad Hatter then maybe she ought to explore more of this Wonderland. Truth be told she was feeling any desire to leave this place so soon. Curse her curious nature...

As she went further into the woods, the way became more darker until much to her dismay she found herself losing track of her direction where she was walking and now had no idea or any clues as where to look. It became clear that her absence mind of admiring the scenery had caused this to happen.

"Oh, buggar me," Alice groaned and rubbed a hand through her hair trying to figure out what to do next.

Then she heard a rustle nearby and Alice looked round frantically. "Oh! Hello? Mr Rabbit, is that you? Or...is that your name anyway?"

Had she been looking behind her, she would have noticed that two sets of large blue eyes were staring at her somewhere from the bushes. Instead of simply just turning round, Alice found herself looking at a fallen hollow log thinking that there might be something in there of her interest and began to get on her hands and knees and start to crawl through it.

But of course if one had noticed a pattern with her so far on this crazy adventure in Wonderland, her fat ass got her stuck once again.

"Bloody hell, why was I cursed with such a massive bottom?!" Alice cried out in frustration and began trying to wriggle her way back up her wide hips had caused a blockage and from inside the log the lovely blonde girl was letting out cries of anger.

It was them during her struggle that the two individuals came out of their hiding spot and stopped briefly to stare at her wriggling to get out of the tree she had foolishly got herself stuck in. Before Alice knew it, she felt a set of hands on her ass.

"Hey! Who the hell is that!" Alice snapped and thought that it was to be another groping incident that she sadly only knew too well.

Suddenly she felt herself getting pulled backwards thanks to those hands and the help from them managed to get her free with a comical 'popping' sound being emitted as soon as she was pulled out from the log and from this it had her landing on her rear to look up at two of the most strangest looking twins she had ever seen. They were dressed in what looked like old fashion school boys clothes with matching bright red caps, ties and dungarees, dull grey undershirts along short and spiky red hair.

Though they looked human, they were very different to anyone Alice had ever seen as they were a short, stumpy and chubby looking pair about half the size of her.

They were standing with each with an arm round the other's neck, and Alice saw that one of them had `DUM' embroidered on one side of his collar, and the other `DEE.' On the other collar on both was the word 'TWEEDLE' and Alice began to think these might have been their names. Then again who would put their names into their clothes?

"I say, what curious names," she said to herself assuming of this theory. "Still as wax-works..." They stood so still that she q uite forgot they were alive and when she stood up towering over them to touch the belly of the one marked 'DUM', she was startled by a honk from him.

"If you think we're wax-works," he said, "you ought

to pay, you know. Wax-works weren't made to be looked at for nothing!"

"Contrariwise," added the one marked `DEE,' "if you think we're alive, you ought to speak."

"I'm sure I'm very sorry," was all Alice could say and began to walk away. "But if you excuse me, I have to go—"

But her way was blocked when the two of them stood in front of her. "I know what you're thinking about," said Tweedledum: "but it isn't so."

"Contrariwise," continued Tweedledee, "if it was so, it might be and if it were so, it would be; but as it isn't, it ain't. That's logic."

Alice was taken aback by what they were saying, even for her this was too curious what they were trying to say. Did they know about her trying to find a white rabbit and getting out off this wood?

"Well I...I was thinking, which is the best way out of this wood as I'm trying to find a white rabbit or someone called Mad Hatter. Would you tell me if you know either of them, please?"

But the little men only looked at each other and grinned.

They looked so exactly like a couple of naughty schoolboys (hence their outfits), that Alice couldn't help pointing her finger at Tweedledum, and saying "First Boy!" Tweedledum cried out

briskly and shut his mouth up again with a snap.

"Next Boy!" said Alice, passing on to Tweedledee, though she felt q uite certain he would only shout out "Contrariwise!" and so he did.

"You've been wrong!" cried Tweedledum. "The first thing in a visit is to say 'How'd ye do?' and shake hands!"

And here the two brothers gave each other a hug, and then they held out the two hands that were free, to shake hands with her. Alice did not like shaking hands with either of them first, for fear of hurting the other one's feelings; so, as the best way out of the difficulty, she took hold of both hands at once: the next moment they were dancing round in a ring.

This seemed quite natural, despite what anyone might think of the scene, and she was not even surprised to hear music playing: it seemed to come from the tree under which they were dancing (some sound speaker they had planted somewhere? Then again nothing made sense here in this strange world known as Wonderland), and it was done, as well as she could make it out, by the branches rubbing one across the other, like fiddles and fiddlesticks.

The twins being chubby would soon find themselves out of breath. "Four times round is enough for one dance," Tweedledum panted out, and they left off dancing as suddenly as they had begun: the music stopped at the same moment.

Then they let go of Alice's hands, and stood looking at her for a minute: there was a rather awkward pause, as the blonde didn't know how to begin a conversation with people she had just been dancing with from barely knowing them.

"It would never do to say 'How'd you do?' now," she said to herself, "we seem to have got beyond that, somehow!"

She paused for a moment then at last said, "I hope you're not much tired?" "No, but thank you very much for asking," answered Tweedledum.
"So much obliged!" added Tweedledee. "You like

poetry?"

"Well... yes...pretty well — some poetry," Alice said doubtfully not knowing where this was leading to. "Would you tell me which road leads out of the woods and find the white rabbit and the Mad Hatter?"

"What shall I repeat to her?" said Tweedledee, looking round at Tweedledum with great solemn eyes, and not answering Alice's question. "'The Walrus and the Carpenter' is the longest," Tweedledum replied, giving his brother an affectionate hug. Tweedledee began instantly:

"The sun was shining "

Here Alice placed her hands in her back jean pockets and ventured to interrupt him. "If it's very long," she said, as politely as she could, "would you please tell me first which road"

Tweedledee smiled gently ignoring her question and began again:

"The sun was shining on the sea, Shining with all his might:

He did his very best to make the billows smooth and bright — And this was odd, because it was
The middle of the night.

The moon was shining sulkily, because she thought the sun Had got no business to be there After the day was done —
"It's very rude of him," she said, "To come and spoil the fun."

Alice was baffled by this random story or what it had to do with anything and she tried to get to the point. "Excuse me—"

The sea was wet as wet could be, The sands were dry

as dry.

You could not see a cloud, because No cloud was in the sky:

No birds were flying overhead — There were no birds to fly.

The Walrus and the Carpenter Were walking close at hand; They wept like anything to see Such q uantities of sand:

If this were only cleared away,' They said, it would be grand!"

What on earth did this have to do with her trying to find her way? "Hello? Are you even—?"

If seven maids with seven mops Swept it for half a year,

Do you suppose,' the Walrus said, That they could get it clear?'

I doubt it,' said the Carpenter, And shed a bitter tear.

O Oysters, come and walk with us!' The Walrus did beseech.

A pleasant walk, a pleasant talk, Along the briny
beach:
We cannot do with more than four, To give a hand to
each.'

"Excuse me," Alice tried to ask politely through
grinding teeth over her failure to get through to them,
but alas...

The eldest Oyster looked at him, But never a word he
said:
The eldest Oyster winked his eye, And shook his
heavy head — Meaning to say he did not choose To
leave the oyster-bed.
But four young Oysters hurried up, All eager for the
treat:
Their coats were brushed, their faces washed, Their
shoes were clean and neat —
And this was odd, because, you know, They hadn't
any feet.

Alice would have ought to have lost her temper now at this rate and given the current situation one couldn't have blamed her for this. She did gaze over towards the trees and had a suspicious that all of this might have all been some set up...

Four other Oysters followed them, And yet another four;
And thick and fast they came at last, And more, and more, and more —
All hopping through the frothy waves, And scrambling to the shore.
The Walrus and the Carpenter Walked on a mile or so,
And then they rested on a rock Conveniently low:
And all the little Oysters stood And waited in a row.
The time has come,' the Walrus said, To talk of many things:
Of shoes — and ships — and sealing-wax — Of cabbages — and kings —
And why the sea is boiling hot — And whether pigs

have wings.' But wait a bit,' the Oysters cried, Before we have our chat;

For some of us are out of breath, And all of us are fat!' 'No hurry!' said the Carpenter. They thanked him much for that.

The young adult woman couldn't help but facepalm at how much of a farce this was turning out to be and that was saying a lot considering how nothing about this world made sense.

'A loaf of bread,' the Walrus said, Is what we chiefly need:

Pepper and vinegar besides Are very good indeed —

Now if you're ready, Oysters dear, We can begin to feed.'

But not on us!' the Oysters cried, Turning a little blue.

After such kindness, that would be A dismal thing to do!'

The night is fine,' the Walrus said.

Do you admire the view?

It was so kind of you to come!

And you are very nice!'

Alice's watery blue eyes gazed up towards the darkening sky and wondered how long she had been standing here for. Had time really stopped and this was purgatory? Oh God, she hoped that wasn't the case...

The Carpenter said nothing but Cut us another slice: I wish you were not q uite so deaf — I've had to ask you twice!'
It seems a shame,' the Walrus said, To play them such a trick,
After we've brought them out so far, And made them trot so quick!' The Carpenter said nothing but

The butter's spread too thick!' I weep for you,' the

Walrus said:
I deeply sympathize.'

With sobs and tears he sorted out Those of the largest size, Holding his pocket-handkerchief Before his streaming eyes.

"Oh, please get this over with!" Alice pleaded; she was fed up with these two.

'O' Oysters,' said the Carpenter, You've had a pleasant run!
Shall we be trotting home again?' But answer came there none — And this was scarcely odd, because They'd eaten every one."

Finally, they finished their nonsensical, stupid and pointless tale which left Alice angered, annoyed yet bewildered at what she had just heard and wonder if some of her IQ must have taken a hit.
What did this have to do with anything about trying

to find her way to look for the Mad Hatter and White Rabbit?

The twins both looked up at her with happy and childish grins that seemed to be waiting for her to praise them for this tale. That said she could barely remember anything about it and had to be careful not to harm their feelings. She picked up in her mind a random scene of choice.

"Well...I like the Walrus best," muttered Alice, "because you see he was a little sorry for the poor oysters...or whoever it was."

"He ate more than the Carpenter, though," Tweedledee pointed out. "You see he held his handkerchief in front, so that the Carpenter couldn't count how many he took: contrariwise."

"That was mean!" Alice said indignantly. "Then I like the Carpenter best — if he didn't eat so many as the

Walrus."

"But he ate as many as he could get," Tweedledum pointed out. This was a puzzler. After a thoughtful pause, Alice began, "Well then, they were both very unpleasant characters—Oh, never mind!"

Here she checked herself in some alarm, she then realised that having spent all this time with the twins that she had most likely not only lost track of the white rabbit but also forgetting the way to where the Mad Hatter was and how dark it was getting with to top all that with no idea where to go.

She began walking angrily away and as she did, Tweedledee and Tweedledum began getting involved in a school yard type argument that only young naughty school boys would get up to which involved lots of pushing and shoving taken place. Alice used the chance to get away from the pair and head deeper into the colourful woods. The blonde woman was starting to wonder if all this time they deliberately weren't trying to help her and instead just waste her time for whatever really simply to make her life difficult.

As she grumbled to herself thinking about her bad luck and what she might encounter next, there was one thought that found herself now having a craving for as hunger was starting to get to her. Her gurgling stomach made itself clear on how it felt.

"Drat...I could kill to have a whole cake now!"

She only hoped that she wouldn't have to deal with those two pests again and that the Hatter, if she so just so happened by chance to actually find him, might be more...reasonable, though judging by his name, she was possible clutching at straws...

Then again, strange things always seem to happen in Wonderland and something in the back of Alice's mind was telling her that this whole madcap adventure was far from over...

CHAPTER 04
THE MAD HATTER

Chapter Summary: At long last, Alice finally meets the Mad Hatter and more than just sparks fly...

As night was starting close in, Alice went walking down a pink gravel path in where she hoped it would ultimately lead her to the Hatter and with nightfall starting to show, she hoped things would work out after many false turns so far in these strange woods. The slender blonde girl really had no idea what to expect with who this person might be; would he be another animal of some kind or something human related like Tweedledum and Tweedledum? Would she find a place to rest for the night (still hoping that the Mad Hatter would agree to it) and what did the Cheshire Cat mean by thinking Alice would be the Hatter's mate?

And the less said about that stupid white rabbit that had gotten her into this world in the first place the better; that rabbit was likely gone by now.

It was all very strange for her to think about such things, mainly annoyed how much time she wasted back there both on the beach on that pointless meeting with Tweedledee and Tweedledum and wonder why didn't she just walk away as soon as she did. She blamed this on her having to be raised to be respectful and not to interrupt whenever someone was trying to speak but surely it really could have been deserving if she had followed her own thoughts there. Nonetheless as she walked along the path, she used the chance to notice some of the wildlife in the woods.

To say the wildlife in Wonderland was totally bizarre would be an understatement as there were flying seahorses with wings on them, badgers with shovel tails and purple horn like duck creatures that swaddled along nearby were just some to name a few. However, the more she went along this path that seemed to be going on to nowhere, she felt her stomach grumble and the pain of hunger struck her.

"I hope this Hatter has something for me to eat," Alice moaned, "that is if I can find him, oh, where should I go?"

Just as she was feeling both annoyed and hungry, Alice suddenly smelt a whiff of something delicious floating through the air that was familiar and something Alice all knew very well.

"Wait...does that smell of...cake? Yes...Yes! It is!" It was said that if Alice were a sniffer dog to

search for cake then she would have been top of the class as she always had a keen sense of smelling for cake as demonstrated in that moment.

Without further thought, she broke into a sprint in the direction of where the smell was coming from while talking to herself as to what kind of cake she might encounter.

About a few minutes later of following the trail, she found herself looking at a tall hedge and beyond that was a kooky yet charming looking cottage which with it's straw roof and patterned panelling look like one of those old houses you'd find in the countryside and judging by how strong the smell was, it was certain that the cake smell was coming from there and this simply had to be the location of the Mad Hatter.

As she was heading towards the garden gate, she heard china plates breaking, followed by a loud row over who was to blame for what had happened and then so suddenly and storming out of the gate was a tall and well-dressed brown Marsh Hare.

He looked really pissed off as he stormed out and didn't even seem to acknowledge Alice being there by walking straight past her while swearing to himself about how that Hatter ruined his prized teacup and how in general, he was an asshole.

Alice stared at the Hare walking away in bemusement for a moment until her attention turned back at who or what was behind that hedge. With some trepidation, she went to the gate and opened it carefully feeling that something was going to suddenly jump out at her; not exactly a wild thought considering what she had experienced so far in Wonderland.

What she found was not only a charming cottage but a beautiful garden that looked like a well- presented garden that was like from one of those stately homes. However, it was on her left she saw a sight that caught her eye...a long thin table covered in a green table cloth with many chairs around with two big red leather chairs on either end and a mix of lovely yet some broken tea cups and pots dotted all over the table. Oh, and not forgetting the many types of colourful cakes to be seen that Alice has smelt out.

"Goodness," Alice muttered with his blue eyes wide, "who on earth would've done this...?"

Her answer was standing on the far end of the table was a man not much older looking than she was, and the man was annoyingly trying to fix his broken tea cup and he must have heard her speak for he whipped round his gaze towards her and Alice got a better look at him.

He had thick brown hair, hazel brown eyes, a long maroon trench coat that to Alice at least looked oddly like those worn by the Beatles on the Sgt Pepper album. He was also wearing matching black trousers and shoes, a lighter red shirt underneath and a black waistcoat on top of that but most important of all...a large red top hat on his head that was tipped slightly at an angle.

It was clear to Alice that this man was the Mad Hatter, or according to the Cat, the lost king of Wonderland. Regardless of those thoughts, Alice was mesmerized by this man in front of her as even though she had just met him, she thought that with his looks and well dressed manner, he looked to be the most handsome man she had ever come across.

Neither of them said a word until the Hatter blurted out with, "a guest! Why do you come here?!" Alice was taken aback. "Oh! I'm sorry if I've arrived unannounced but I was—"
The Hatter suddenly leapt up onto the table with grace and began running along the table while somehow avoiding damaging any of the plates, cups and pots over until he kept off the other end

and landing right in front of her not only did she get a more closer look at his handsome features but was greeted by a strong masculine musky smell from the Hatter and boy didn't it smell as good as cake!

"Who are you?" Asked the Hatter, his accent sounding refined yet all over the place. "You don't seem to be from here."

"Well, no I'm not," Alice replied while trying her best to not give into her urges thanks to that smell from the Hatter which seemed to be getting stronger. "My name is Alice and I'm from Scotland...y-you do know where that is, right?"

Hatter gave her an odd stare, then he began to eye her up and down before then pulling her close by putting both his hands on her ass and giving it a sq ueeze. Alice would've tried to get out of this situation before hand, yet she found herself stunned into amazement as she felt a wave of electricity running through thanks to his touch and nearly let out a moan of pleasure.

Alice couldn't tell what was this mad yet wonderful

feeling rushing through her as the Hatter suddenly broke into a manic grin. "A human from the upper land! Come we must have tea and cake—oh! And we simply must celebrate your unbirthday!"

The Hatter dragged Alice by the hand (his touch feeling so soothing to her) and led her to one of the red leather chairs for Alice to sit on. It was only then Alice got a better look at this chair in which seemed very shiny, like PVC, had comfy looking armrests giving the impression of a ornate throne and to top it off it had gold swirl lining on it.

Then she sat on it...Alice practically sank in it and the feeling felt so good. She wanted this chair whatever happened to her now, probably the best chair she had ever sat on which might have sounded a strange thing to say but it was that good and as she wriggled her rear on it to get comfortable, the chair was sq ueaking a lot and for some reason that was turning her own.

Maybe she was growing madder by the minute? However suddenly she realised that the Mad Hatter looked like someone she remembered when she fell down that rabbit hole...the man in the portrait! she felt foolish not thinking of this sooner the moment she had seen this man though another thought occurred to her as to who the blonde woman in that portrait was. Was it really her and that portrait of them looking old was a vision of the future? Then again given how strange things were in this world it was a possibility and she sat there closing her eyes in enjoyment as she sat on the red leather chair.

"You seem to like that chair," the Hatter noted with a grin and who was now sitting at one of the table chairs alongside her to start pouring tea.

"Certainly I do," Alice moaned softly, then remembered something. "Goodness! I forgot to ask you your name, is it really the Mad Hatter?"

The Hatter gave her a plate and teacup. "I prefer King Hatter if you don't mind...I am the true heir of Wonderland if you knew that—please have some cake!"

"Thank you," Alice replied by grabbing a slice of pink cake nearby and gorging down on it very un-lady like, something that the Hatter noticed with amusement.

"My, my! You must be mad like me to have a whole slice like that!" The Hatter laughed standing next to her. "I thought humans were more orderly."

Alice wasn't listening; combined with the Hatter's handsome looks and smell, a very comfortable

chair and this cake which was probably the best she'd ever tasted...she was more turned on than she'd ever felt before in her life.

"I was raised to act like a lady," Alice replied as she rubbed her belly with satisfaction, "but I really don't care for that, I never felt like I fitted in with that world and wanted a world of my own."

The Hatter beamed that smile again. "Then it would seem my dear Alice you have found such a world! You do sound mad enough to fit around here!"

Upon him calling her 'his dear Alice', not only did Alice's underwear get positively soaked for what seemed like the millionth time that day, but she was now feeling strong and attractive feelings for the Hatter. How was this happening all of a sudden though?

"Well I...I suppose I have," Alice muttered. "But you haven't said about who you are."

The Hatter's cheerful expression q uickly changed to one of regret. "Me? I'm the last of the Hightops...the true rulers of Wonderland."

"What happened, Hatter?" Alice asked. She knew a bit thanks to the Cat, but she wanted to get the Hatter's take on it. "A long story," Hatter sighed sadly. "My family rule Wonderland for well over 700 years, until one day about a hundred years ago my father's sister, the Queen of Hearts, led a coup to overthrow the Hightops and place herself on the throne. I'm the last of the Hightops left."

Alice was speechless, what a horrible fate to suffer though there was something that bugged her... "Hatter, what'd you mean a 'hundred years ago?' You look...young."

"I'm 437 years old," Hatter explained as if it was no big deal. "Or 27 years old in human years. Time is slowed down here once you leave Earth."

It was a random but nonetheless interesting fact

about the Hatter and Wonderland. However, she had more q uestions. "I'm so sorry what happened to your family...but what kind of name is 'Hatter?'"

The handsome brunette smiled. "Not my actual name...I go myself by the name of 'Hatter' by two meanings. One is that my royal name is hard to speak in any language the other is my hat...this is not just a hat, but a crown of the Hightop kings and q ueens."

So that explained why he had that hat, but Alice let her hand rub his larger hand gently. For some reason it felt right. "I hope you do regain your kingdom and become the true king of Wonderland."

"But only if I find a suitable q ueen," Hatter added, his eyes now looking warm and loving. "I only have a chance to reclaim Wonderland if I have someone to rule with as part of Hightop tradition." Alice felt her breathing began to get heavy, she did not know if he was trying to hint at her or not, but her heart was hammering hard. The sexual tension in the air was so thick that you could cut it with a knife, and both were silent until a rustle could be heard in the bushes behind Hatter.

"That bloody bird again!" Hatter groaned and rushed over towards the bushes to try and clear the whatever it was.

As he was over there and he did his business to sort out the bird, Alice was feeling
now really turned on; every one of her senses was active. She watched the Hatter with longing and placed a finger by her mouth and two other fingers inside of her as she began to play with herself fantasizing about the Mad Hatter.

Oh yes, in that moment see was starting to realise that she was falling in love with the Hatter, but

how? She had only met him about a few minutes ago

and she was already wanting him to fuck her brains out and that was not including the fact he was actually a different species to her; maybe she really was going mad?

By the time the Hatter returned, Alice was cleaning off the juices off her fingers and stared lovingly at him. "Come on my dear," Hatter said. "It's getting late, I can find you a room if you like in my cottage."

Even just the way he spoke made her feel at ease and he truly did have a golden tongue. Suddenly as Alice tried to stand up but she could not. She was stuck to the chair and the sq ueaking got more noticeable as Alice moaned and struggled to get up.

"Alice? What's wrong?" Hatter asked.

"How do I know?!" Alice snapped. "Why am I stuck...? Oh, God not again!" Her fat, juicy ass had gotten her stuck in that chair!

"Oh, that blasted bottom!" Alice moaned in embarrassment.

Seeing her struggle, the Hatter went in to help her by grabbing her sides and after much wriggling from Alice, she was pulled out of the chair with a 'popping' sound and landed right on Hatter's chest were that certain smell of his had become more pungent.

She pulled away with her arms round his neck and the Hatter's arms around round her waist. No words were said, and they stared into each other with pure intimacy, passion, and sexual tension until finally their lips suddenly smashed upon each other's and it became a hardcore make out.

Tongues wrestled for dominance, the Hatter grabbing Alice's fat ass and the horny blonde girl began grinding into the Hatter in which she could feel that the Hatter was getting an erection and that combined with the wave of pleasure rushing through her that was sending her over the edge.

They broke away for air with a trail of saliva connecting their mouths and took in for some much-needed breath.

"Come on Alice, my Queen deserves to be treated well," the Hatter purred, and he led Alice into his kooky cottage and up to his bedroom to take their sudden new relationship to dizzying heights.

After a mad rush to the bedroom and the Hatter had thrown his coat and hat to the side in which after some directing towards the bed, Alice found herself on top of Hatter. She began to unbutton his shirt to reveal, much to her delight, a very hairy chest and hairy body underneath.

(Alice always had a thing for hairy chests than muscles.)

The blonde began to kiss her way down his chest until she got to his waist and began rubbing her hand over his bulge. "What are you waiting for, Alice?"

Hearing that was all she needed to unzip him and for to come face to face with a large, thick tasty looking cock which popped out at once the moment it was exposed.

"Good lord it's huge!" Alice gasped yet she wasted no time in placing it into her mouth and giving him the blowjob of his life.

"Mmm, all mine," Alice thought lustily

It was all new territory for them, yet everything seemed to be perfect with the Hatter moaning with pleasure and Alice loving this feeling right up to the point in which the Hatter released his load and Alice's mouth was soon full of his own seed. All of which wasn't bad for her considering she had never had any sexual relations prior to this anf for her first it was truly incredible.

"Well, you tasted positively delicious," Alice slurred, her gaze droopy and the Hatter laughed. Before she knew, both went into another make out in which by the end of it, both were naked, and the Hatter loved the feeling of her smooth and sensual skin on his own. He then flipped her on her back with the Hatter straddling himself on top.

"Now my dear Alice...prepare to be taken by a Hightop."

With those words, the Hatter slipped his throbbing cock inside of Alice in which she cried out in pleasure and loved the feeling of the Hatter thrusting into her. Nothing could top this; she had not only found the man of her dreams but the place where she wanted to stay. As the hardcore fuck took place, Alice felt her gaze go emerald green and her eyes glowed green as did Hatter's. Little did she know what this was whenever a Hatter was about to climax such as he was, this meant that Alice was being 'marked' as Hatter's territory and that no one else would be able to claim her except for him.

"Oh god, Hatter!" Cried Alice as she felt herself about to lose herself after about five minutes of her lover thrusting in and out of her soaking wet pussy.

It finally ended with both screaming out their climaxes as well as Alice being filled and covered all over with the Hatter's load before finally both fell onto the bed sweating and breathing heavy from a truly magnificent romp.

"Well, that was a fuck worthy of a king," Alice panted, her gaze returning to normal from the green colour.

"And you are worthy to be worshipped by all in Wonderland," the Hatter replied softly as he began to spoon her as their naked bodies got under the covers. "I will say you are also the most beautiful girl I've ever laid eyes on...Lord you are everything to me, more than tea and cake even!"

The horny girl grinned at his words and she sighed happily of the thought that she had had her first time and she knew that if she were to return to her world, no man would ever give something like that ever again and this Hatter was not really human after all.

It was then Alice made a monumental decision that would decide her fate. "Hatter...I wish to stay with you and in Wonderland. Forever."

"You mean that?" Hatter asked, his voice with hint of hopefulness.

"Oh yes," Alice purred. "I could never go back there after the delightful experience I've just taken. How can I go back after all this?"

"And I couldn't be happier and mad about it," Hatter grinned and began kissing down Alice's smooth back though her fat rear pressing up against his penis, it wasn't hard for it to get hard again and the blonde girl giggled at this feeling and started to playfully grind on it.

That said though despite what might be the start of another romp, the two of them, mainly out of pure exhaustion, both fell asleep shortly afterwards while holding each other close. Whatever the future held for Alice and her new life in this crazy world, one thing was for certain was that now she would be a permanent resident of Wonderland and just end up a little bit madder now.

CHAPTER 05

THE TULGEY WOOD

Chapter Summary: After deciding to stay in Wonderland forever, Alice decides to explore the nearby Tulgey Wood though it turns out that going there might've been a bad idea...

Alice woke early the following morning but kept eyes shut for fearing her fantasies would end up being ruined and for good reason after what she felt had happened.

"It was a dream," Alice groaned in her 'sleep'. "All just a wonderful dream...I found myself in a strange land called Wonderland and I found a man who was going to supply me with comfort, cake and lots of sex...why can't I have good things?"

Alice knew she had to wake eventually and slowly opened her eyes fully expecting to be back in her flat in Marchmont Edinburgh and get ready for yet another dull day trying to look for work in the hopes that she could finally tie a job down; why did life in general had to be so boring? Her blue eyes only got wider when she saw she was not in her bedroom but instead a kooky, Victorian style looking bedroom that she recognised as Hatter's bedroom. Her heart started beating fast realizing that this was not a dream but was in fact real and the incredible sex she had last night was far from some wild fantasy of hers.

It was a wonderful feeling for Alice that told her for once that life was not being cruel to her and she removed the silky maroon bed sheets to reveal her naked body underneath and quickly found herself covering up as if someone was in the room but alas there wasn't.

Then the memories of her fantastic fuck with the Mad Hatter that truly had been one of, if not, the best feeling she'd ever had. Speaking of which where was Hatter? Alice's thoughts were answered when stepping into the room shirtless with only his black trousers and red hat/crown on his head was her handsome Hatter and in his hands was a tray featuring a cup of tea and plate of a lovely whole pink and white cake that to Alice looked just as tasty as Hatter.

"Morning my dear Alice," Hatter grinned before handing over Alice the tray. "Breakfast in bed my dear."

The blonde-haired girl looked on wide eyed. "C-cake for breakfast?!"

"What is it? Something wrong?" Hatter asked with concern evident in his eyes.

"No-no of course not," Alice stammered. "I mean, I love cake but...this is certainly not like where I come from, just toast or cereal in the morning you get."

The Hatter raised an eyebrow and chuckled. "Well then, seems you need to know more about Hightop culture. Always cake for breakfast, lunch and dinner and did I mention many tea parties?"

"Oh my, that does seem like a luxury life but...will I gain weight from having just cake?" Alice had been concerned about her weight and although to many people looking at her would see that she was a slender and attractive looking woman who had no signs of being fat, her fears of putting on a few pounds thanks to her cursed love of cakes was always something that made her frustrated that could affect her. Her signs of doubt did not go unnoticed by Hatter who had something to say about that.

"What a mad notion my dear! Look at me!" The Hatter chortled by showing of his slim body. "I have only ever had cake and unlike your world, we don't include the ingredient that makes one fat, why do you folk in the Upperland do that? Seems a rather silly thing to include if it ruins the meal, maybe you are all mad up there?"

Oh yes, there were many mad people up where she came from and Alice could not deny that one bit, though perhaps not what Hatter might have thought about it. Nonetheless hearing about that she wasn't going to gain weight from what was looking like a cake-only diet from now on was all Alice needed to hear, within a matter of a few minutes she had practically devoured the whole cake leaving just a plate of crumbs in her wake which made even the Hatter amazed at the sight of how q uick of a job she had made of the cake. "Heaven's you are mad like all of us! You do belong here with all of us!"

The horny and greedy girl did not listen to the Hatter's words as enjoyed the sensation of tasting perhaps the best cake she'd ever had and that was only ever making want to stay in Wonderland even more.

"My darling Hatter," Alice purred as she began

drinking the eq ually lovely tasting tea. "You have made this a most exceptional breakfast fit for a q ueen."

"Just how I intend to," Hatter replied softly and leaned down to give her a soft kiss and the kiss became q uite a passionate one that Alice nearly dropped her cup of tea onto the bedsheets.

After they pulled away, Alice then got up and found a fluffy, blue housecoat by the bed which was not there before and Hatter chuckled at her confused reaction.

"Made it just for you," Hatter added in which Alice gave him a raised eyebrow.

"Such high service," Alice replied with feigned amazement before putting it on. "Now then, it appears I need a wash, where is your bathroom?"

The brunette Hightop let Alice slip her arm into his

own as he led her towards the bathroom. "This way my dear and funnily enough, I'm needing a wash too..."

Alice was then shown the bathroom and despite its vintage yet cartoonish look, it looked so luxurious with there being a huge bath that looked more like a jacuzzi; all fit for a King and Queen no doubt. Boy, if this wasn't making her turn her back on her own world then what would?

The two of them ended up sharing a bubbly bath together in which their naked skin would be touching each other and drove them crazy until their bath time ended up with having sex which that

seem to last four seemed like half an hour. More things for Alice to love in Wonderland.

Eventually, Alice got dressed in her usual jeans, blue camisole and short sleeve white blouse that Hatter had washed, cleaned and even fixed a few wears and tears it had previously, though Alice swore that her jeans seemed to hug her curves more as well as making her ass look even bigger than it actually was. Oh well, Alice did like the comfortable feeling her clothes felt now and those hands of Hatter could seem to do almost anything wonderful...

For the rest of the morning Alice spent that time enjoying life in the cottage. Hatter had brought in the big red leather chairs into the sitting room in which in that moment the two of them were having a peaceful time together with the Hatter making tea and cake while Alice was comfortably sitting in what she now called her 'red leather throne' while reading a book on the history of Wonderland.

Seeing her sitting there on the chair with a legged cross sipping a tea in one hand and reading a book in the other she looked very much like a proper lady and she really felt right at home. The whole cottage had a rather cosy feeling with the walls being of a warm beige colour, a fireplace nearby burning nicely in the corner, many bookshelves surrounding the walls and much of the furniture looking q uite old yet nonetheless classy in many ways. A far cry from the bland and modern look of the apartment she lived in back in the Upperland and Alice had always loved humble looking places like the look of Hatter's cottage and in some ways was little wonder why Alice was wanting to stay here.

Being the curious girl she was, Alice was fascinated by the history of this strange world, how you were able to get to the Upperland and had found out more about Hatter's species and to her astonishment saw them closely related to rabbits! It read that in Wonderland rabbits had grown to become the dominant species out of many of the races which talked and they had grown into humanoid form and had lost much of their rabbit form. So Alice thought about that her lover was pretty much just a human rabbit? How curious indeed...

But then she remembered about the white rabbit and the book had stated that there were races of rabbit that hadn't changed though went up to the Upperland to explore and it became clear about why the only way into Wonderland was via a rabbit hole. She was glad to know more for her curious mind to think about, but it was was a page on a place known as the 'Tulgey Wood' and how it was alleged to have some of the strangest animals even for Wonderland standards.

Not surprisingly, she was wanting to know more as she did with that lovely cake she had for lunch.

"Hatter my dear," Alice called over to her lover, "what is this Tulgey Wood I hear about that makes it so curious?"

Hatter's eyebrows furrowed. "Why do you ask? It's

the woods nearby this house."

He then pointed over towards the dark woods nearby and Alice's gaze widened. "I say, I didn't really notice it when I came here. I'm in the mood now to explore more my dear Hatter..."

Upon hearing this proposal, Hatter crossed his arms. "Alice, you do know that there are animals that can even eat you up if you're not too careful. I don't want anything bad happening to you my q ueen."

Hearing him call her 'queen' made her feel giddy and Alice, after sipping the last of her tea and placing the cup in its small plate on the armrest, walked over to him and planted a big, fat juicy kiss on his lips.

"But my king, I will be careful. I have done well already since landing in Wonderland." She turned to leave through the doorway before looking over her shoulder to stop. "Besides, I need your magnificent cock to fill me up for my supper. I can't stay away for long, my dear."

It was then for Hatter to feel rather excited as he felt an erection take effect in his trousers and q uickly bounded over to Alice to grope her ass with one hand and the other play with her breast all the while kissing down her neck.

"Wouldn't want any harm to come to you my dear," Hatter purred as he kissed down her neck with Alice moaning in satisfaction which concluded with Alice getting her fat ass spanked by Hatter who added with, "take care, Alice."

With a quick kiss, Alice left the house and headed towards the Tulgey Wood while Hatter stared longingly at Alice's butt as it shook while she walked. Hatter really did want to fuck this amazing girl soon as possible. It was then his attention was alerted to something large and orange bounding away and disappeared into the woods. It was that bird that Hatter had to chase away the previous night and he q uickly suspected that bird might be out to cause trouble.

"I better give a q uick word to Albert," Hatter pondered and began to make a plan...

Meanwhile and oblivious to this, Alice ventured deeper into the Tulgey Wood and admired that despite how dark the place was thanks to the tops of the trees blocking out the sunlight, the woods seemed to glow thanks to the teal and maroon coloured trees that seemed to cause a glow that helped illuminate the woods.

"Such curious way of lighting," Alice admired as she looked around. "This certainly wouldn't be allowed back in−"

HONK!

"Oh!"

She stepped on something sq uishy and made a loud honking sound as it happened. Looking down she thought she saw a family of ducks until she noticed that though they had duck feet, their bodies were that of a large purple car horn with two googly eyes by the horn/mouth. The one she had accidentally stepped on made many angry horn noises at her before heading towards a pond with the other duck-horn animals.

"It was only an accident," Alice muttered before carrying on seeing what else she could find. After going down a pink dirt path, she came upon a red tree that to Alice's amazement had what seemed like dozens of signs giving out directions saying such things such as 'Here, 'There, 'Down', 'Up' and 'Back' just to give a few examples.

"Such a strange way to show the way, some poor fellow might get lost," Alice tutted, though truth be told by that point she was rather confused herself where she was going. She would head left and didn't know that from up in the trees there was a small creature which looked like large red, rounded glass with stick legs, a pointed carrot nose and two little green eyes near the bottom of the rim of the eyes which looked more like glasses.

The group looked on at this girl they had never seen before and one of them decided to go in for a closer look by jumping down onto Alice's shoulder that she never felt it land. The little creature then planted itself over Alice's face and soon her vision became a weird kaleidoscope effect that caused more confusion for her.

"Goodness! What on earth is...?" She figured out that the glasses were trying to hypnotise her and would have done so had she not removed the glasses creature q uickly from her and placed it by the branch of a tree. "Not the time for nonsense, well, bit difficult to say that in a place like this."

Running by her feet was another bird animal that had the body of a green parrot though it's head was none other than a large pencil head and it began writing the word 'Nowhere' on the side of a tree.

"Well then, that explains a little bit," Alice muttered q uietly randomly before moving further on.

She then came by a waterfall and saw what seemed to be a group of umbrellas standing under it. Just then she took a second glance and saw that on top of what should have been a pointed object were in fact many bird heads and it was then that Alice realized that they were more strange animals.

They glared at her as if she were in their territory and that she shouldn't be here thus Alice q uickly got the hint and headed further on. Next, she came across a butterfly, though like everything not all was as it seemed and the wings were like two pieces of bread.

"Such a fascinating place," Alice sighed as she sat down on a rock to admire the woods. "I could get lost in here and find more curious creatures, though I might not find Hatter again... oh, how I could have him now!"

Just even thinking about him simply turned Alice on like crazy not just in his handsome looks but so too was his mad personality that she found extremely attractive, oh, and his hairy chest and magnificent cock just to add as the cherry on top.

Alice began to get wet again and slipped her fingers into her jeans to play with herself and her moans might have been heard from around the forest and one certain animal did but for all the wrong reasons that Alice was about to find out. It was the bird that had followed her all the way from Hatter's cottage to here and it was a large bird about a few feet taller than her thanks to it's long legs as well having orange feathers around it's body, a red mass of fuzz on top and a large beak that could take anything in it.

However, what this bird creature had was a large bird cage body that could fit a person in it and judging by the way the birdcage bird drooled at the sight of the horny and tasty looking blonde girl known as Alice, it had its mind set on who it wanted inside of it. From the moment it saw Alice finding the cottage, it had never seen such a delicious looking girl and would surely be a well deserving meal for it and hopefully take her away deep into the woods were she'd never be seen again by anyway but only itself.

Using the chance while she was in her own world engulfed in pleasure, the birdcage bird crept up towards her slowly and q uietly in which by the time Alice finished with an orgasmic cry of joy and her juices splashed about, the bird opened its giant mouth and Alice didn't have a chance to react as she looked up as when she did, she found her view covered in darkness and cried out for help which unfortunately for her those cries were muffled out.

The giant bird lifted her up from the rock she had been sitting on before leaning its head backwards to try and swallow her whole while she kicked her legs trying to escape. For Alice, her cries of terror began to turn into cries of pleasure as she oddly found the sensation of being eaten alive rather sexy and she began to ejaculate inside the bird's mouth.

"Oh, why was I born so horny?!" Alice moaned in both pleasure and annoyance as she didn't know if she should escape or accept her fate as bird food while all the while enjoying herself.

While half of Alice's body was in the throat, her lower half was stuck at the entrance of the mouth thanks to her fat bottom. Was it really for once that her large ass was about to be useful to get her out of a sticky situation?

Alas, no. Instead, thanks to her juices acting as a lubricant in which the bird tilted his head backwards in which helped swallowing the girl down in one gulp and Alice became a bulge sliding down the birdcage bird's throat until she popped out the entrance to the cage headfirst in which she landed on her head and lay there dazed at what had happened. Of all the times in which Alice would have liked her bottom to get her stuck for once, it sadly wouldn't work out for her this time much to her own annoyance.

She would come to her senses thanks to the bird letting out a satisfying burp and Alice looked round and realizing to her horror that she had been swallowed whole and much a normal budgie she knew, she was trapped in her own prison.

Only in Wonderland could such a thing happen to a person.

"No! Let me out you disgusting bird!" Alice cried out, hitting her hands on the bars. "I can't be your dinner; I have a life!"

The Bird though was not listening and satisfied with is delicious meal it began to run deeper into the wood with its catch.

"Let me out! Someone! Hatter!" Alice cried as the bird ran before not long later went to its nest to rest while on the inside, it was dawning on Alice that she was, like any bird in a cage, possibly trapped in here forever and worst of all... a bird's meal.

"No...this can't be how it ends," Alice uttered in disbelief. But there was nothing she could do. Then for some reason the whole feeling of being eaten seemed to make Alice horny and both out of feeling annoyed at her potential end and turned on being trapped in a tight place in which she could only sit, she began fingering herself.

The birdcage bird seemed annoyed at her moaning not to mention that her juices made her even more wet than before. Nonetheless even though the bird could not digest her, it seemed satisfied with it's tasty catch and now how on Earth was Alice to get out of this one? Would she ever escape or was she to become nothing more than a permanent addition to the Tulgey Wood?

One thing was for certain, things could always change so easily here in Wonderland...

CHAPTER 06
FROM THE JAWS OF DEFEAT

Chapter Summary: *After ending up in the belly of a bizarre bird creature, Alice gets help from an unlikely source...*

Alice was trapped. That was all that could be said about her current dilemma though how she was trapped was something that not even in her wildest dreams she could have dared thought about.

Why was that? She had been gobbled up by a large birdcage bird creature and now she was trapped in her small prison in which not only couldn't see stand up being forced into a sitting position but that she had no way out of this strange prison and was possibly to be stuck in there for what looked like a long time to come.

Her curious nature had really gotten her into trouble this time!

At first Alice had, rather bizarrely, found the whole feeling of being eaten a big turn on but after half an hour trapped inside this birdcage in which she could barely move, she began to feel bored by it all. The only consolation to all of this was that she had not been digested as it seemed the bird didn't seem capable to do that.

How was it to eat without digesting its food made Alice ponder this curious q uirk about this strange bird but quickly gave up as trying to think of any rational thoughts in Wonderland was a foolish idea, maybe it could yet it had a slow digestive system and was yet to start and that sleeping might be the way to activate it? Alice then thought about the book she had read about the history of Wonderland and tried to recall what this bird was called how it was to deal with it's food.

By this point the bird was resting on its nest and was fast asleep while during all this time Alice had been trying to think of a way to get out of her prison. She had suspected like any cage there was a lock to open, but she could not find anything like that. Then again it dawned on her that this strange bird didn't seem to have anyone to either piss or shit it's digested contents out; surely everything that went in must ultimately come out? The blonde couldn't help but giggle at a thought of the thought of this bird shitting her out unharmed and not covered in faeces which sounded ridiculous, but then again this was Wonderland of course...

Along with thinking about how this bird worked, she had even tried to pull apart the bars around the cage, but despite their thin and weak looking appearance they were as tough as iron and she was starting to give up on trying to escape and thus accept her fate as bird food; a bizarre end to her life that she never thought was possible. Though speaking of birds, she heard someone whistling cheerfully nearby and looking over to where it was coming from and when she saw who was whistling she couldn't believe who was walking along the path.

It was the Dodo from the beach she had met when she first arrived in Wonderland and from she could see, he looked to be in a rather good mood and then wondered if maybe...

"Oh, Mr Dodo!" Alice called out q uietly as she could as to not to wake up her captor.

The Dodo grinned as soon as he saw her and ran over to greet Alice. "Ah! There you are silly girl!"

"Can you get me out?" Alice asked hopefully as she leaned forward and gripped the bars with both her hands. "I've been trapped here for goodness knows how long and I don't know what might happen to me."

"Why of course," the Dodo agreed as he rubbed his

hands/feathers together. "Though on two exceptions."

The blonde woman raised an eyebrow. "Like what?"

"First thing," the Dodo began, "why did you leave while we were on the beach?"

Alice rolled her blue eyes remembering the encounter. "Well, I was looking for a white rabbit... actually, I totally forgot about him." She paused remembering how it was all because of that rabbit she had ended up in this strange world. "But I felt what you were trying to do back there was utter nonsense."

"But it worked did you know!" The Dodo retorted. "That race was a success, plus nonsense is my middle name!"

"I can understand that" Alice muttered darkly, still

annoyed that she was nowhere close to getting out of this prison.

"Now then," the Dodo added. "Can you try and guess my name?" "The...the Dodo?" Alice asked not sure. "Nope! Wrong there you silly girl!" The Dodo exclaimed. "Try again!" "Um...Fred?" "Nope."

"Bobby?" "Try again."
"Geo—No, Fredrick?" "Good guess but try again." Alice groaned placing her hands on her face at how hopeless this situation was for her. "Sir, does this have to do with me escaping?"

"Of course, it does," The Dodo. "King Hatter told me he wants his good lady to be brought to safety."

"Wait, how'd you know about me and Hatter?!" Alice stuttered.

"The good king found me as he suspected you were going to end up in trouble and it looks as though he was right."

Wait, did Hatter plan a rescue or was this just some strange coincidence...? Oh, what did she

know? There was no point in q uestioning such things in Wonderland. Still, she had to try and figure out the name of the Dodo.

"Alright then Mr. Dodo," Alice sighed. "Is your name Wilhelm?" "Try again."
"Is it Marcus?" "Nope. "Albert?" "CORRECT!"

Alice nearly jumped out of her skin at the Dodo's cry. "So...your name is Albert?" "Indeed, you are correct dear, Alice," Albert nodded.

Alice was confused. Albert? That was the Dodo's name? After what she had found out in this strange world, that name just seemed so...normal. But then another thought crossed her mind. "But...Albert...how do you know my name?"

"King Hatter told me everything," Albert explained. "Mostly how you are now the possible future Queen of Wonderland and your voracious appetite for cake...lots of cake. Good heavens I don't want to think about that. If I was to have all that cake I might make myself sick!"

As she heard this, Alice smiled that she could be a queen and giggled at Albert's reaction of her love of cake. "Anyway, could you please get me out of here?"

"Well course my dear," Albert nodded. "Allow me to work my magic."

He stood back and Alice watched on with curiosity at what he was planning to do. He then cleared his throat before clapping to get the giant bird's attention.

"I say you there! WAKE UP!"

The birdcage bird made a moaning sound as it woke up, clearly sounding droopy and not happy from being awaken from its slumber. Though Alice couldn't get a good look, she could possibly tell that it was glaring down at the Dodo.

"Don't give me that look for I am here to help you," Albert scolded before looking inside his jacket pocket to pull out a small bottle that to Alice looked like the bottle that had shrunk her when she first got into Wonderland.

The birdcage bird's long neck leaned forward to get a good look at the small the bottle that Albert was holding up for it and it was here that Alice could just see on the side of the bottle that it had a label on it that read 'sniff me'.

("That's easy for any crackhead to follow," Alice thought sarcastically to herself.)

"Yes, please do smell it for I feel you'll rather enjoy it!" Albert stated and opened the lid to allow the giant bird to get a sniff of the stuff and the contents seemed to be like pepper, and with pepper, that could surely mean one thing how Alice might be about to get out of this...

"Please don't be what I think it is," Alice gulped.

The birdcage bird sniffed it and then suddenly it gasped leaning its head back while making difficult breathing sounds.

"You silly old buffoon! You weren't meant to sniff it all up!" Albert tutted though he gave Alice a wink at what was to come.

Then suddenly as the birdcage bird acted like it was about to sneeze by the gasping it was doing, Alice felt herself being lifted as if she was being sucked up like a vacuum and it all became clear that this was only going to end one way...

The birdcage bird let out a mega sneeze with such force that Alice felt herself being sucked up through the throat with Albert seeing an Alice size bulge making it's way up before be blasted out of the mouth (for once her large bottom had not got her stuck) before tumbling through the air to land upside down with jean cladded bottom on full display for was in such a tasty position to spank her ass with glee.

That said she didn't mind this for the fact that crazy Dodo had gotten her free from her prison!

"Come my dear, we must go!" Albert cried motioning at her to follow him in which she self- righted herself to get back on her feet before rushing behind him to wherever it he was leading her. Alice glanced back as she ran seeing the Birdcage bird lying on its backside looking dazed at what happened before shaking its head to witness its tasty meal running away.

Without warning it took chase and even though both Alice and Albert had gotten a head start, the long legs of the birdcage bird were helping it to close to gap on the escaping pair.

"He's getting close!" Alice cried out and fearing she was about to become a meal for the second time that day.

"Not for long though!" Albert replied. "There is a path of mushrooms over there that will help you escape!"

"What do...actually, just show me," Alice groaned. If she got out of this, she was wanting to have a long wash, eat cake and have lots of sex with Hatter once again after the mad day she had found herself in.

Then again if she was to become a permanent resident of Wonderland then she would have to realise that misadventures would become the norm for her and this was only her second day in Wonderland.

After a few more sharp turns later, Albert and soon led her towards the pile of mushrooms he had been talking about and what she found was a cluster of them in a radius of about five foot wide and Alice did not quite understand how this was supposed to help her escape. As she took the chance to look at them, they were giant red mushrooms with white spots on them as well as having thick white stalks on them and while they looked like what one would think about mushrooms there was something different about them in which Alice couldn't put her finger on.

"Are you sure about this?" Alice asked in confusion as she gazed with suspicion at the mushrooms.

"Of course, silly girl!" Albert snorted. "All you have to do is jump on the mushrooms and you'll be able to get out of here.

"You mean like...take me somewhere else?" Alice asked placing her hands on her hips with suspicious thoughts.

Albert paused waving his head slightly in thought. "Umm, more of less I suppose." Then came the sight of a charging, hungry and terribly angry birdcage bird making a beeline towards Alice. "No

time to explain just do what I say, goodbye!"

"No wait!" Alice shouted but the Dodo had made a run for it into the bushes and Alice's eyes widened in horror as she saw her previous captor rushing towards her and looking like there was no other way to get out of here other than what Albert had claimed.

"Shit, shit, shit!" Alice cried and knew she had little choice as the creature was getting closer and could do nothing other than leap onto the mushrooms.

What happens next stunned even her. In a millisecond, many thoughts flooded her mind as to what was going to happen to her. Was she going to sink through the mushrooms and be trapped within? Would she be teleported somewhere else? Would the mushrooms end up being like one of those carnivore plants that as soon Alice stepped in she would be eaten alive like a fly? If that was the case then there was no doubt she would be digested unlike that birdcage bird.

What happened all took place so fast. With a comical bouncing sound that one would expect to hear in a cartoon, Alice found herself being launched through the air at great speed up through the trees and out of the Tulgey wood. Alice had been stunned at what had happened to her that she didn't noticed that she was high up in the air and when she did notice, she was falling and tumbling down though the air and Alice screamed thinking this was it and that she'd rather been bird food that end up following that stupid Dodo.

She closed her eyes as her whole life seemed to flash by her eyes, her childhood, High School, her good for nothing parents, going down the rabbit hole and finding Wonderland and falling in love with Hatter. Why was what in her uneventful and boring life had to end like this just as when her life was starting to look for her. Then came the landing and at the point her life must have ended here. Instead, she found herself landing on something soft, comfortable and sq ueaky... something that felt familiar to Alice...

To her amazement she looked round to see she had ended up back in Hatter's front garden and that she had landed in her favourite red leather chair.

"My my! You certainly know how to make an entrance," Hatter chuckled as he helped her up (with some trouble thanks to her getting stuck in the chair, again.)

Alice felt a bit flustered. "Did you...know I'd land here?"

"A Hightop has to plan ahead my queen," he replied. "It seems that the Dodo found you am I right?"

She nodded and Hatter carried on speaking. "I knew you might find yourself in trouble when I saw that ruddy bird follow you into the woods and thus, I had to contact my good friend—Mmph!"

He was cut off mid-sentence when Alice wrapped her arms round his neck and smashed her lips on his to show her gratitude.

They seemed to lock lips for a whole minute which

include tongues battled for domination, Alice grinding into her lover and Hatter feeling an erection coming on. But then they heard a cough to get their attention and Alice realised there was a third person there and as she pulled away Alice saw sitting at one of the chairs by the table was a familiar brown Marsh hare rabbit that Alice remembered leaving Hatter's garden just as she was entering.

"You've already forgotten about me, Hatter?" The Marsh Hare asked in annoyance as he drank a mouthful of his tea.

Hatter though smiled and wrapped an arm round Alice's slender waist and looked over at him. "Come on now, Fredrick. I told you I would introduce you to Alice and here she it!" He paused and looked over to the blonde girl. "Alice my dear, this is Fredrick one of my good pals and hopefully you'll get to know each other."

Alice tilted her head at this...Fredrick, and didn't know what to think about him. He looked ruffled with his clothes having the appearance as if they had been dragged through dirt and his golden eyes had that of a unkind and short tempered individual. "Um, how do you do, Fredrick," Alice greeted trying to sound polite as possible.

"You two seem to fuck a lot," Fredrick drawled boringly as if he was talking about the weather and Alice's face flushed red. "Just from the way you look at each other I tell you Alice seem to like it up the arse, am I right?"

Hatter's eyebrows furrowed. "Freddy! Don't you dare speak to your future Queen like that! She will demand our respect and love from the people of Wonderland!"

The marsh hare waved a hand away half-heartedly, "yeah sure whatever. It just so happens that whenever we get a human ending up in Wonderland that human just so happens to end up with one of the few people in this world that looks remotely human. When do the rest of us get any luck?"

Alice pondered about the thought and even though she thought Fredrick was rude she could somewhat understand of him being jealous of Hatter and also wonder how on in the world Hatter seemed to be friendly with him. Then a thought came to her about to try and please Fredrick.

"Um, about what you said there," Alice pipped up, "there are a group of people where I'm from known as 'Furries'."

Both males gave her a curious look as Alice carried on speaking with, "they are q uite a mad breed themselves. always have a thing about dressing up as animals and some even like to have, well, do certain stuff in bed with animals so if one of them ended up in Wonderland..."

Part of her cringed at the Furries. She knew all the negative stuff about them as anyone who dared looked at the dark side of the internet would do and she had no doubt in her mind if one of them ended up here with it being a place of talking animals who acted like people then they would have a field day here. But she shook the thought away from her mind and weirdly neither Hatter or Fredrick seemed that bothered by what she had to say.

"They sound boring if you ask us," Fredrick remarked and Alice never thought that anyone would say that about Furries, but then again this was Wonderland when things that seemed strange up there were perhaps normal down here.

Then Hatter placed a hand on Alice's cheek to help turn her gaze over to meet his warm brown eyes which made her all giddy and that comforting smile on his lips seem to ease any fears she still had after her madcap experience. "My dear Alice...you've had a long day..."

He then began to slowly leave a trail of of kisses down her neck and Alice moaned softly as he did this as her underwear began to get wet again. Then she felt his hardening errection and she couldn't help herself as she smashed her lips on him as she wrapped her arms around his neck while Hatter placed both hands on her jean cladded bottom and sq ueezed it tightly making her moan during their passionate kiss.

So passionate was their make out was that both had forgotten about Fredrick sitting there who looked more mildly annoyed at things by rolling his eyes looking away while drinking his tea as if seeing a couple making out in front of him was the most boring thing in the world.

Then after about a minute of their lips being locked

and their tongues wrestling for dominance, they pulled away and a lustful look now in Alice's eyes as she could only mange to say a few words as follows. "You. Me. Bed. Sex. Now!"

And he did, Hatter then lifted her up into his arms to carry her bridal style and without another word he led her up to his room and left Fredrick sitting there almost forgotten about.

"What bloody cheek!" Fredrick groaned and promptly stood up and walked away from the garden wondering whatever might happen next. One thing was for certain that with Hatter now having a woman in his life, Fredrick knew that things weren't going to be quite the same again for Wonderland. Meanwhile for the madcap couple, they fucked for the rest of the day with the screams of pleasure from their sex being heard by anyone who was near the cottage. Such a mad day it had been for Alice for she had q uite literally escaped from the jaws of defeat, surely things could not get madder than this? Truth be told and little did she know, they would in due course...

CHAPTER 07
A WILD TRIP

Chapter Summary: The time has come for Hatter to begin his mission to overthrow the evil Queen of Hearts, but not before Alice and he end up having a wild trip in more ways than one.

To say Alice was living a life of fantasy would be putting it nicely. In the two days since she had fallen down that rabbit hole in which she found Wonderland and ended up staying with Hatter Hightop, aka the true king of Wonderland, her life had changed for the better in her opinion.

For all her weirdness that made her something of an outsider to many when growing up in Edinburgh, she had found out that in this strange world that not only did she fit into this place but also felt like she was born to live out the rest of her life in Wonderland with Hatter. Oh yes, had it already been mentioned that she was loving her life here?

Every night and morning had evolved a lot of cake

and sex, a perfect mixture for Alice if her now crazy and mad life was going to be like this from now on. During that early afternoon, she and Hatter were snuggled up on a red leather couch with Alice resting her head on Hatter's chest and hearing the different pattern of heartbeat there (different because he was a different species from Alice) and the two were happy just to be lying there content at the current situation. Alice would have liked to have gone out and explore the world but it was rainy outside and there was nothing they could do but just relax indoors though to be fair after the madcap moment that that hungry bird in teh Tulgey Wood maybe it was just as well that the rain stopped her from going anywhere today.

As intimate this moment looked, the Mad Hatter was thinking and looking at the window as the rain pelted it and thoughts drifted to him about the future of Wonderland and the throne. Oh yes, he may had been mad as what they all called him, but he certainly wasn't a man without a plan and in that moment as he looked down at the stunning blonde woman in his arms, one mad idea came to him.

"My dear... I think it's time to retake the throne," Hatter announced to Alice and she rose her head up to look at him.

"I'm sorry, what?" Alice inq uired.

"It's time to overthrow the Queen of Hearts and reclaim my rightful place as king," Hatter explained. "Now that I have someone to be there with me, we can finally end that mad Queen's reign once and for all!"

"Now? But what are we going to do? Do we need an army or something?" "Mmm, haven't fully worked it out but I'm sure it'll work."

Alice rolled her eyes, of course he'd say that as he

was, well, mad. It was in his character to do things on the fly and sometimes this would lead to him not thinking things through. Nonetheless she wanted to help Hatter take what was rightfully his and if it worked out, not only would Hatter be king, but Alice herself would be q ueen. That thought alone always got her excited in more ways than one.

Suddenly the Hatter gently pushed Alice away and stood up to adjust his clothes, though he felt something in his pocket and remembered something else he had to ask Alice which was probably just as important than retaking the throne.

"Alice, before we go there is one more thing to ask of you."

"What is it Hatter?" Alice inq uired but she gasped when the Hatter got on one knee and brought out a silver ring from his pocket.

"Alice Kingsley, will you be my wife and queen of Wonderland?"

The blonde girl clasped her hands over her mouth and felt tears in her eyes and she only had one thing to say. "I...I... YES!"

She didn't need to say anything else; instead she crashed her lips on his and a hardcore make out took place which lasted about half an hour and ultimately ended up with Alice given Hatter a blowjob. An elaborate way of saying 'yes' but not that Hatter was complaining as when he climaxed his seed filled Alice's mouth and she moaned licking every last drop of it.

After they got back on their feet, Alice slipped on the ring onto her finger and smiled at her new fiancée. "Oh, Hatter...I cannot wait to be your wife and q ueen when that time comes."

Funnily enough by the time their madcap love making was finished, the rain had stopped and with that it was time for them to go. The two then walked away hand in hand as Hatter led the way to wherever they were going to. For Alice, she had time to reflect on the situation and thought about her immediate future; she had only known this man for a few days yet was suddenly engaged to him. It was mad, then again, so was this whole world in general.

There was a sense of irony for Alice as she would always find it silly in these Disney princess films that the girls got married after hardly knowing the prince (Alice especially thought that Princess Anna in the film 'Frozen' was a total whore for getting engaged to someone she just met) but now after all that time finding all those relationships silly, Alice now found herself in exactly that same situation.

Alice though did not want to think of the hilarious irony of it all, logic never really applied to

Wonderland, so this might have been normal plus she felt such a physical and emotional bond to Hatter it was incredible, where was she going to find someone like him in her life? Certainly not back where she had come from that was for certain should she do the unthinkable and go home. Home for Alice was now Wonderland.

As the couple walked hand in hand through the woods and admiring the views and chatting excitedly to each to each other like any newly engaged couple, they then they heard footsteps behind them and the sound of a gruff male voice muttering angrily of why it had to be him and all sorts. Looking round it was another creature about a head shorter than Alice. It was a green lizard with big tennis ball sized yellow eyes and wearing a grey flat cap with wearing workman like clothes while carrying a wooden ladder. Whoever it was Hatter seem to know who it was.

"Ah Bill! How it is my good man?" Hatter greeted cheerfully, but the lizard walked past without even noticing the couple and still muttering angrily. "Oh dear, he's not in good mood today." "What's wrong with him?" Asked Alice.

"Knowing Bill it could be anything," Hatter replied, "come one though, let's find out."

As Bill the Lizard was on the same path as they were walking down, it didn't take long until they managed to find him outside a charming looking cottage that looked a lot like Hatter's home and in the front garden of this home as Bill was walking up was none other than a certain white rabbit who was looking flustered.

"My goodness it's the white rabbit!" Alice pointed out to Hatter excitedly. "He was the one I followed down the rabbit hole to get here, something about being late or something."

"You mean Tobias?" Hatter inquired.

"To-who? Tobias?" Alice asked in confusion.

Hatter pointed out the rabbit in question. "That rabbit there is called Tobias. He's always been late for something, never good with keep schedules and all that."

Alice stared in bewilderment. She should have known better that the rabbit should have had a name like anyone, still she had gotten use to calling him 'White Rabbit' that knowing his actual name was just a strange thing for the blonde to ponder. As she mulled her thoughts over this, an argument had broken about between Bill and Tobias with the former towering over the rabbit and complaining loudly.

"You're due to pay me for the work I did for you!" Bill demanded, clearly it seemed to be a past event that

Alice was unsure about.

"Oh dear I've been awfully late on so many things that I've forgotten about that!" Tobias quivered looking fearful.

The lizard though was having none of it. "Don't give me that you lazy good for nothing prick! I want my money now!"

"But I haven't got it I swear!" "I want it now!"
"But Bill I mean it!"

Then it all happened. In something almost like a comedy movie in which a chase happens, that was what happened next as Bill starting chasing the terrified rabbit around the house. Alice felt that if the Benny Hill theme could be played it would have fitted the scene taking place before her and would have found it hilarious had she not felt a little bit sorry for the rabbit. Hatter on the other hand grunted, shook his head and clearly had seen enough.

"Well, I think we should stick out of the way and let them sort this, um, debate." With a playful slap on Alice's ass, they carried on walking down the path where they went further into the woods. It was a peaceful walk in which the couple couldn't help but grin at each other and clearly loved each other and in one random moment Hatter's hand, which had been placed on Alice's back, slipped down towards her rear in which he squeezed it and this made the blonde sq ueak with surprise.

"You cheeky devil!" Alice spluttered but her fiancée laughed.

"But you clearly like it when I do it though, huh?"

"I can't confirm or deny that," Alice muttered q uietly with a blush.

Just then they heard a chuckle from the treetops and they both looked up behind them and from the darkness there seemed to be someone up there and something about that laugh seemed to be familiar to Alice.

"Well what'd you know, it's him," Hatter muttered to Alice. "Come down there, Cat!"

The thing emerged from the treetops and there was a certain Cheshire Cat who floated downwards to get level with the couple. That famous large grin of his only widened at putting two and two together and seeing the ring of Alice's finger confirming that they were indeed a pair.

"Well, well, well, it seems that things have rushed rather quickly for you two," the Cat laughed. "How do you know about this?" Hatter q uestioned. "Were you spying on us?"
"On the contrary," Cheshire Cat grinned as he floated

around them in a circle. "I saw your good lady friend in the woods and merely directed her to find you and thus...it all seemed to have gone rather well don't you think?"

"It's true," Alice admitted holding onto Hatter's hand. "I didn't know what to expect until I found you."

"It would seem then am I matchmaker don't you think?" The Cat boasted by tumbling forward while he was floating. "Does this mean I'll be the best man, or rather best tom, at the wedding?"

The brunette man snorted. "Don't get any bright ideas you little..."

But the Cheshire Cat had gone. The couple looked around and could see no trace of that cat. He had pretty much vanished into thin air

"You realise that some are madder than others here," Hatter sighed in annoyance. "More than most?" Alice replied raising a suggestive eyebrow.

Hatter rolled his eyes and allowed Alice to wrap her arm around Hatter's arm. "Come on my dear, there is much to do."

They walked for quite a long time through the woods with by now Hatter placing his hand on Alice's ass (again) and gently squeezing it; always something that Alice really enjoyed from Hatter. By now they had gotten towards the opening of the woods and around them there were giant mushrooms about the size of a house and in the distance was the first sight of what looked like the palace.

"There is my home," Hatter happily pointed out to Alice.

The palace wasn't all that big compared to other castles Alice had seen, but it had a whacky look, colourful and something that looked like out of a cartoon in which seemed to be keeping with much of what Wonderland had to offer.

"A most marvellous palace," Alice smiled. "But if you don't mind me asking...how are you the last of the Hightops?

The Mad Hatter's expression turned solemn. Alice had read a bit on how the Queen had overthrown Hatter's family and how she had beheaded the king and q ueen, yet there was a mystery as to what happened to the rest of the family.

Hatter sighed. "Well then, what those history books fail to mention is that the Queen has a pet... a deadly pet called the Jabberwocky."

"What is a 'Jabberwocky?'" Alice asked with a great deal of curiosity.

"The most horrendous creature to set foot in Wonderland," Hatter explained. "It is a giant dragon creature that can smell flesh and can devour you if you find yourself with it."

Alice shuddered remembering how that birdcage bird had made a meal of her and how she had just managed to get away from it. How many creatures in Wonderland could eat someone? She knew she'd have to be careful.

"No one knows where the Jabberwocky came from," Hatter continued, "though wherever the Queen found it, that monster has been used to hunt a eat all the Hightops that got away...all except for me."

The long blonde-haired girl gasped and quickly embraced Hatter. "I'm so sorry Hatter. But why are you doing it now after all this time of sitting in the shadows?"

He smiled warmly at her. "I always promised I had to find a future q ueen before attempting a coup. Now that you're here, we can do it, but we must be careful."

"What can we do to defeat the Queen?" Alice asked, curious about the prospect of taking part in a coup d'état.

"There is a weakness," Hatter explained. "It's the Jabberwocky itself would you believe. For some reason to make it serve her, the Queen put a curse on it that also pretty much controls her army. If the Jabberwocky is killed, then her influence is finished, and she will be overthrown."

It was q uite a lot for Alice to take in, but just as she was going to ask more q uestions that they had a sound coming from the Woods and the Hatter immediately dragged Alice into the bushes.

"Quick!" He said, "it's the Queen's troops!"

Hatter and Alice hid behind some thick bushes as the sound of marching feet could be heard coming down the pink path. It didn't take long for the troops to reveal themselves as to Alice's amazement were two lines of walking deck of cards with hands and feet either red or black as well a small head on top.

"Goodness, what a curious platoon," Alice whispered to Hatter.

"They are technically mine," Hatter added, staring intently at them. "Bloody mad Queen stole them from me." Then one of the guards looked up and stared towards the bush, he had heard them!

Quickly the engaged couple ran further into a field of giant mushrooms to hide. Alice looked back to make sure they were not being followed and thankfully they were not but unknown to Alice, Hatter spotted something, or rather someone, in the distance.

"It's him! Look!" Hatter cried.

Alice looked back in front and there sitting on a large mushroom while smoking a hookah pipe was a large blue caterpillar with numbers going down one side with shapes and patterns on the other side. It was an amazing sight but by this point all the strange things that with all what Alice had seen she was probably used to it by now.

As they got by the base of the mushroom the Caterpillar had taken a whiff of his pipe and looked down at the couple immediately knowing the Hatter.

"Oh, the lost king of Wonderland," said in a bored tone as if had gotten bored of this fact previously.

"How do Bertie!" Hatter greeted happily with a manic grin that suited his personality to the ground.

"Is all good my loyal subject?"

"All very well," the caterpillar, supposedly called Bertie, replied dryly before then noticing Alice standing there, "and who are you?" The Caterpillar said those certain words with shapes of letters raining down on Alice, making her cough.

"I'm...I'm Alice."

"You don't seem to be from here," Bertie noted by her appearance.

Hatter then pulled Alice close. "Indeed, she is not. She is my fiancée and the future q ueen of Wonderland."

Hearing that made Alice smile at the fact of how much Hatter thought of Alice. However, Bertie did not seem fazed at this news. "You can never keep your emotions tied down can't you, Hatter? You do know that even if you succeed in taking down the Queen of Hearts then you two would have to produce heirs to keep your bloodline going."

Alice's eyes widened as the thought of having children dawned on her. She hadn't thought about the importance of having an heir if she was to become queen and this wasn't including the fact she and Hatter were different species, then again given the amount of times they had fucked already she had to wonder if maybe they had conceived already and she might be carrying said child...half human half whatever race Hatter was.

She never thought she could be a mother, she always didn't really think about it nor even thought that she could ever be a good mother, yet for some reason the thought of her having Hatter's potential children was a weird turn on for her. The again it seemed that anything evolving Hatter always did that for Alice.

Hatter then spoke up again. "Come on now, Bertie. Give us a whiff of your pipe, always good to have a pick-me-up in the afternoon!"

Wait, were they about to have some sort of drug? Alice's only experience with drugs was with some shitty brownies during her high school years that were a botched job which was something she did not want to think about with the horrendous headache she had suffered afterwards.

Would this be any better? Surely anything seemed to work in Wonderland no matter how crazy it might have sounded to some.

"Fine...very well, have a seat," The caterpillar sighed pointing at the smaller mushrooms nearby. He did not look so happy to share his space with these two.

They both sat on the mushroom chairs, or rather, Alice sank on her one due to her large ass. Weirdly no one seemed to be bothered by this as Bertie started passing round his hookah pipe. Hatter would take a long intake of breath of the stuff first before then Alice drew in a whiff and did the same.

Her whole world seemed to turn on its head as immediately her vision became both glossy and hazy and her senses all over her body were feeling so good.

"Oh God this feels hot," Alice slurred as she began rubbing her hands over her body and especially on her curves before looking other at her fiancé. "Hatter...you look so handsome."

"And you look so fuckable," Hatter drooled as he staggered over to help Alice up.

The blue caterpillar watched with some disgust as the two of them began a long, steamy make out, kissing each other fervently with Hatter rubbing his hand over Alice's ass and she in turn rubbing her hand over his cock which was now getting hard. Neither of them seeming to care that Bertie was watching all this in front of his own very eyes.

"Excuse me," Bertie ordered, "will you please listen?"

The couple were now on the ground with Hatter lying on his back with Alice on top still kissing like there was no tomorrow. They were clearly on one hell of a wild trip that made them unable to listen to anything going on around them.

"Am I just talking to myself?" Bertie snorted crossly and soon realise that he was fighting a losing battle to get their attention.

The caterpillar eventually gave up when the two began to fuck doggy style with Alice bent over with her hands pressed on the stalk of one of the big mushrooms with her pulling her jeans and panties down with Hatter thrusting his cock into her well lubricated pussy.

Bertie then made a final snort of disgust then sprouted wings and flew away while muttering degrading things about 'young people' like Alice and Hatter.

He had to wonder how these two were supposed to be fit and proper rulers of this land should they ever come to the throne. Then again, the lost king was called the Mad Hatter for good reason.

Alice and Hatter moaned as their fuck session approached its climax in which Hatter screamed with pleasure by ejaculating his load into Alice and the two fell to the ground exhausted and still giddy from the hookah pipe.

Neither of them did anything while lying on the ground, let alone notice that the caterpillar was gone, but it would be Alice while still in a haze, stood up, pulled up her cum soaked jeans and staggered away towards the palace not even fully realising that she was leaving Hatter behind...still with his large, throbbing and sticky cock exposed for the whole world to see.

Hatter's drugged effects wouldn't last long as he was more use to the stuff, but when he came to his senses he saw that Alice was gone and q uickly suspected she must have gone towards the palace and with that...trouble.

"Oh drat," Hatter sighed, "better get the gang together to help me out. Where are Albert and Freddy when you need 'em?"

Further away from Hatter, Alice staggered her way towards the palace almost if she was drunk and it would be another few minutes before Alice's drug effects would go away, but thanks to her curiosity and her body telling her otherwise from her mind, Alice was about to find herself in a world of yet more trouble. In some ways, staying there with Hatter and keep on fucking might have been a safer option. Little did she know just what trouble she was about to find herself in...

CHAPTER 08:

MEETING THE QUEEN

Chapter Summary: After awaking from her drugged state, Alice ends up at the palace and with it, comes face-to-face with the Queen of Hearts...

Still in her drugged state, Alice had pretty much no idea where she was going other just walking down some long pink gravel path towards some way out from the Woods. It was only after about ten minutes after she had aimlessly walked away from Hatter was that her hazy vision started to go away and realized she was nowhere near the Woods but in fact facing in front of her was an exceptionally long and neatly trimmed hedge.

"Goodness," Alice gasped, "wherever must I be?"

Taking a few steps back and seeing towering over the hedge was the wonderful looking palace that upon getting a better view of it up close made it seemed like something out of a cartoon and the brick work Alice swore she could tell had some strange patterns on them as if the brickwork was faint heart shape patterns built into the design, a curious bit of design she had never q uite seen before. By this point however it was clear that this whole world seemed to be one big cartoon in of itself and she must have been the odd thing out in this strange world.

As she pondered this fact, she remembered that drug she and Hatter smoked and their crazy sex season that followed that during it. A sexual romp which led Hatter cumming inside her though being drugged she was unaware of it though and if she did she would not mind anyway knowing that it was her fiancé. Call her shamelessly bias but she felt Hatter could do no wrong.

Alice looked around again and much to her dismay was that Hatter was not there and that the combination of being drugged yet having her curious nature on show had ultimately led her to be lost and she had no one but herself to blame for that, though in fairness that caterpillar might had to share some of the blame.

"Oh bother, now what?" Alice pouted as she placed her hands on her hips.

As she was trying to figure out what to do next, she heard someone muttering from behind her and her heart leapt thinking that Hatter had found her, though looking back she not Hatter but someone else who rushing towards the hedge. A certain someone in which Alice only knew q uite well who it was and was the culprit for leading her into this crazy world to begin with; someone who wore a waistcoat and was a rabbit...

"Mr Rabbit!" Alice cried out as she followed him, but then she remember from her fiancée that the rabbit had a name. "Oh, Mr Tobias! Or is just Tobias? Please don't run away I need a word with you!"

Tobias wasn't paying any attention and was looking flustered with only one thing on his mind. "I'm late! I hope the Queen won't have my head, oh why is it always me?!"

With Alice hot on his tail (literally) she managed to just catch a glimpse of Tobias' face and she was shocked to see that he had a black eye. He never had that when she last saw him though she remembered the confrontation he had gotten himself involved with Bill the Lizard which had ended with the latter chasing the poor rabbit round his house. She didn't know who would have won the fight though she noticed his neatly presented clothes looked ragged showing all the evidence that he had been in a fight and yes, her curiosity was wanting to know more.

Though as Alice followed him through a gap in the hedges into what seemed like the entrance into some kind of maze, there was something worrying her about what Tobias had said regarding him losing his head at the hands of the Queen. Surely Hatter was only exaggerating about what the Queen was like? Right? Then again giving how everything in this world seemed to be all crazy, he might have not been exaggerating but telling the full truth.

After going down a few wrong turns and thinking for one moment that she had lost the white rabbit, again, she found him standing proud holding a small bugle in his hand and with that now also wore a white tabard with a heart in the centre. Before she could say anything, she noticed that he was standing next to a white wooden sign that in red letters read 'Royal Croq uet Game'.

Alice had played some of Croq uet during her childhood thanks to her parent's rich hobbies in all those garden parties and she did actually rather enjoy it so this might be something up her street. But then she remembered about wanting to speak to Tobias.

"Oh, Tobias, I finally found you!" Alice sighed with relief.

The rabbit stared at her with suspicion, his black eye being more noticeable here. "I say, have we met before?"

Alice shook her head, "no but I did follow you the world above and I fell down a rabbit hole. Surely you heard about what happened, right?"

Tobias seemed more interested in something else and cleared his throat.

"The games will be starting soon; you mustn't be late, or the Queen will be mad!" The white rabbit replied with a degree of fear in his voice.

Alice raised an eyebrow at him. "Well, ok...if you say so. I only was wanting a chat, how hard can it be?"

She then wandered into a large garden with trees of lovely red roses blooming from their branches and the smell from them was wonderful and she had always loved flowers because of that. Then as she looked closely at one of the branches of red roses, she realised something was off with them. A red drip followed from one of the roses and it was soon revealed that they were in fact white roses that someone had painted red, but why?

Alice's answer to that would be revealed not far from her in which the culprits for painting the roses were down to three card soldiers who at this moment in time were hurriedly painting one tree while arguing to each other over who was to blame to planting the wrong sort of tree.

Ever q uite a curious girl who could not keep her nose out of other people's business, Alice ventured forward to find out more. "Excuse me?" She asked and the three card soldiers stopped their bickering and stared at her with bemusement at who this strange blonde girl was. "Why are you painting the roses red?"

One of them, a black three of spades, answered with, "you see luv, we planted the white roses by mistake."

"And the Queen only wants them red!" Added the two of spades. "If she finds out, she'll have our heads!" Cried the ace of spades.

Alice gasped, Hatter wasn't lying about her as to was Tobias' fears about all this and now even Alice was starting to feel scared about this mad Queen and that Hatter was not going over the top with how he described her. "Goodness! I'm terribly sorry for you but...where is the Queen?"

Just then from out of nowhere, Tobias appeared blowing his bugle along with a ground of card soldiers following from behind and soon surrounded the garden.

"Make way for the Queen of Hearts!" The rabbit cried and the three card soldiers panicked, threw away their paint gear and fell to the ground bowing while Alice hid behind one of the trees with her heart beating hard as she felt something horrible was coming this way.

"Introducing her royal highness...the Queen of Hearts!" Tobias announced and stepping forward from behind was a large woman dressed in a black and red dress along with a fat ugly face, black hair and a silly small crown that seemed according to Alice was like one of those crowns that Anime princess characters would have. Though she didn't say anything knowing that it might be wise to do just that though that said Alice thought that this woman was not only the fattest woman she'd seen but also the ugliest.

Strangely enough her shade of red and black was similar to that of Hatter's outfit which seemed to make Alice think that red and black were the royal colours of Wonderland. Though in Alice's mind, only one person in the whole of Wonderland seemed fit to wear them...

The Queen gave off an aloof presence and turned her nose up at many who dared to look up at her...that was until her face changed to fury and she stomped over towards the tree Alice was hiding behind and she feared that she had been spotted, however it was one of the red roses that caught the Queen's attention and saw it was dripping red paint onto the ground.

She rubbed a finger on the dripping rose revealing the real white rose underneath and she turned back at the three cowering card soldiers on the crowd who were likely feeling that their doomed was already sealed.

"Who's been painting my roses red?" She asked with tranq uil fury before exploding with, "WHO'S BEEN PAINTING MY ROSES RED?!"

The three soldiers all started blaming each other to save their necks, quite literally, but the Queen wasn't having any of it as she cried out her following orders. "OFF WITH THEIR HEADS!"

Alice could only watch in sympathy as the poor three card soldiers were dragged away begging for mercy to try and get away from their doomed fate, alas there was nothing for the blonde woman could do to save them other than make a silent pray to them and hoped some miracle happened to them. Alice's gaze then turned over towards the villainous Queen and even though she had only seen this large woman for less than a minute, she already knew why many feared her.

Just then the Queen grabbed the trunk of the tree and

ripped it from the ground with q uite amazing strength before throwing it away and revealed a shocked Alice who's hiding spot had been compromised and she was now frozen to the spot out of fear not knowing how to react. The Queen glared at this woman with bewilderment mainly over her strange clothing that was not like anything she had seen in Wonderland.

"And who might you be?" The Queen asked with suspicion.

"W-Well, um, I'm...I'm Alice Kingsley," the blonde-haired woman stuttered in reply. "I hope I'm not interrupting anything?"

Suddenly, the Queen of Hearts smiled as if something dawned on her and her previous foul mood seemed to vanish in a split second. "Ah, young girl! I believe you are here for the Royal Croquet match? Everyone else has pulled out, no clue why with them all saying that they are all busy or one thing or the other, stupid them."

Alice thought for a moment, suspecting as to why people might have pulled out to begin with though it didn't her long as to figuring out why that might be but nonetheless Alice decided to play along if it was to try and get on the Queen's good side. "Um, yes...that is—"

"Excellent!" The Queen boomed happily and began making orders at her soldiers. "Begin preparations for the croquet match! We have found a contestant!"

As the remaining troops scattered round getting things ready, the Queen begin sniffing and gave Alice an odd look. This made Alice react with, "I swear I washed myself this morning. Do I really smell?"

"Oh no my dear nothing to do with that," assured the Queen as Alice lifted up and arm as she sniffed her armpit. "I'm sure you did just that, though I just can't help but pick up a scent from you that I haven't smelt in years, just can't think where though..."

Alice's blue eyes widened, she had learnt from Hatter that whenever one of his species found a mate, aka her, they would not only have sex but also cover their partner in a scent that would see them 'marked' as a claimed partner. Had the Queen found out about Hatter being nearby and his connection to Alice and speaking of which, where was Hatter? Alice could really use his help to get her out of this situation.

"Tell me girl, where are you from?" The Queen asked raising an eyebrow at her.

The blonde's blue eyes darted from side-to-side trying to figure out to explain her mad adventure. "Well, I'm not from Wonderland. I'm from...up there."

The Queen glanced up at the heavens then stared back at Alice. "Up there? As in you fell from the sky?"

"Not quite," Alice replied as she fidgeted with her hands. "You see, I fell down a rabbit hole and ended up in Wonderland. Sounds strange I know."

Just as the Queen was about to reply to that statement, Tobias appeared and cleared his throat to get their attention. "Your majesty, we are ready to begin the game."

The Queen gave Alice one last suspicious stare before going over to the bag that Alice assumed held the clubs. She would be proven to be half right in her guess as they were clubs but not as what she expected. What the Queen pulled out was not a club but a frightened and bewildered pink flamingo that was sq uawking like mad wanting to get away.

"Shut up you stupid animal!" The Queen snapped

and forcefully stretched the poor flamingo into the position of a straight club in which it cried out in pain.

If that sight alone of that poor flamingo being tortured was not horrible enough for Alice, things only got more disturbing when the Queen brought out the ball which turned out to be a small green hedgehog like creature being forced into the shape of a sphere. Then with a great whack, the poor creature was fired through the wickets which turned out to be the card soldiers were using their bodies for that purpose and to say that it looked ridiculously rigged was not even worth to say it was an understatement as the cards/wickets moved for the poor creature being made to roll through all of them in order for the Queen to win her game.

Alice was utterly livid. If there was something she hated more than those in the Upperland who never understood her was cruelty to animals, and what the

Queen did made the blonde woman hate this vile person more than anything she'd met in her life. Little wonder why Hatter wanted to overthrow her over than just for the throne though Alice did have to suspect if these poor animals were being abused, how many more were and what would they being forced to do? It was a horrible thought that Alice only wanted to put an end to it somehow.

As much as Alice wanted to give that woman a piece of her mind, she had little choice other than forcing herself to repeat the horrible action herself as it was now her turn to play the game. Alice wasn't thinking straight for she was very angry about this wicked game and she went to whack the poor rodent with great force but wildly missed it while bending over that much that the sound of ripping was heard from all.

Laughter erupted from all around and Alice did not know what was going on until she placed her hand on her bottom and to her horror, she felt that the seam on the back of her jeans had ripped revealing the silky teal underwear that Hatter had made especially for her for the world to see.

Curse her fat ass to cause her problems at times like these!

Combine this with the animal cruelty she had seen, Alice finally lost her temper and directed her anger at the Queen of Hearts. "You are a truly awful, mean spirited, cruel and bad-tempered overgrown child that is not fit to rule!"

Everyone stopped laughing and gasped in horror with the Queen stunned then growing anger gripped her face with a long and drawn out silence followed, the sort of silence that you would have heard a pin drop.

"Oh bollocks," Alice uttered in horror as she clasped her hands over her mouth as not only her big bottom had gotten her into trouble but so too had her big mouth now pretty much sealed her doom and a fate much like those poor card soldiers was awaiting her.

The Queen's face was going redder by the second with an eq ual furious expression that was looking fit to burst her face apart. "No one, and I mean no one ever calls me that unless they wish for death...OFF WITH HER HEAD!"

Alice was suddenly grabbed by two card soldiers by her arms and dragged her towards the castle. Oh, wow couldn't she had just kept her mouth shut and just go along with it like she had thought of before? Luck never seemed to be on her side though as she was being dragged away, she found an unlikely ally.

"Your majesty, please give the girl a fair trial!" Called out Tobias and much to Alice's amazement, the Queen ordered her troops to halt and she stood there pondering about the req uest and seemed to considering it. Alice held her breath hoping that she might just have a small chance that she could get out of this situation. No one said anything, then...

"Mmm, very well then," the Queen replied with a nod. "The girl shall have a trial, albeit a small one just so I can get what I want... LET THE TRIAL BEGIN!"

Alice breathed a sigh of relief that she had a chance, a rather small and poor chance though. Once again though as she was been forced into the castle and even taking in more of the castle design, she could only mutter at her own foolishness that had gotten her into this mess and where was Hatter? He could not still be out there in the woods still in a drugged state with, dare she suspect, his large cock on full display for the world to see?

She needed to find a way to get out otherwise Alice was going to lose her head. It was one of great irony of that after all these years she had put up with those perverted boys in high school try to grope or spank her bottom, she now felt she'd rather rather be in that situation instead of the current situation she felt she was about to suffer the same fate as to what those poor car solders had obviously suffered. Life could be so cruel at times and her options seemed low.

She was needing a miracle, but how?

CHAPTER 09

ALICE'S TRIAL

Chapter Summary: After calling her mind at how horrible the Queen of Hearts is, Alice finds herself on trial and all looks bleak for her, unless anyone can save her...

Talk about hard luck stories; at the start of the day when Hatter proposed to Alice about taking her hand in marriage all seemed wonderful, now she was about to be put on trial for her crimes for calling out that bitch known as the Queen of Hearts with the punishment looking to be a beheading. All just a normal day in Wonderland. It had been about half an hour since she was taking away and had been placed in this stone prison in the depths of the castle and all she could do was sit and wait as what she had been told that they had to find, or rather rope in, an audience to be used for the trail. And to top it all off, her jeans still had that embarrassing rip up her seam that they wouldn't let her fix it.

Not surprisingly, Alice was fuming about her everything had transpired and was deeply regretting leaving Hatter back there for had she not wandered off she would have avoided this. Speaking of which, where was he?

"Oh, this is hopeless!" Alice groaned placing her head in her hands, "if only I had just kept my mouth shut and played along with the fat bitch then I wouldn't be in this place!"

Before she could think about anything else, she heard a chuckle from somewhere and at first Alice thought it was one of the guards having a laugh about something, but then the more she heard it then the more is seemed to sound like she had head it before, but where? Alice looked around the room and the laughter seemed to be coming from the small bar windows above her and Alice q uickly stood up on the bed to see what was going on.

"Hello? Who's there?" Alice called out through the bars but then nearly jumped back in surprise when on the other side of the bars from out of thin air was none other than the Cheshire Cat was floating in mid air and who was grinning happily at Alice with that trademark grin of his.

"Good afternoon, Alice!" The Cat chuckled, "my goodness you have gotten yourself into a right pickle here, am I right?"

The blonde girl pouted. "Never mind that, get me out of here or else I'm done for!"

"Not so easy there I'm afraid," Cheshire Cat admitted. "I can't get you out here for I'm on your jury and this might compromise things."

"Oh, joy," Alice replied dryly, but the Cat wasn't finished yet.

"But fear not dear Alice for your knight in shining armour is on his way to rescue you with a proud army that will finally end the mad Queen's reign of terror!"

"H-Hatter? He's coming? And...and how's big the army?!"

The Cat began counting with his claws. "Let's see...there's King Hatter then...then...there's Albert, who else now...? Oh yes! There's Fredrick and...well, that's it really."

A long silence followed from Alice, then: "Three? This grand army is made up of three people?"

She knew her fiancée was mad, but then again she didn't expect him to be that mad to go in so undermanned. She felt herself banging her heads against the window bars but Cheshire Cat wasn't finished just yet. "Don't doubt the Mad Hatter so easily, Alice. Things will turn out better than you might expect... Mmm, I think it's soon time, good luck!"

Before Alice could say anything, the Cat vanished into thin air and from behind her she could see why he had vanished. The door of her prison unlocked and two card troops entered and eyed here with contempt.

"Come on lass, move it!" One of them barked at her and Alice had both her arms grabbed and she soon being dragged out of her prison and onwards to her trial and pondering just how she was suppose to get out of this situation.

As they went further up away from the dungeons and into the castle proper, she used the moment to take in the surroundings of the castle interior and she was struck that despite how grand it all looked as one expected from a castle, there was a humble and cosy look about it; one that seemed rather familiar to that of Hatter's home. As a matter of fact, it was almost if someone had copied Hatter's home into the castle but then again Alice remembered that this castle was suppose to be his and maybe he had based his current home on the castle?

Along the walls however were large portraits of the Queen of Hearts all with some pompous pose which only added more to how Alice thought that not only was this woman was horrible but who's vanity was off the charts. A pity though for had it not been for those stupid portraits then this castle would be a nice place to stay in...

After many different corridors later, Alice was finally dragged into the courtroom which had a roof that seemed to go towards the heavens and the room seemed so large in general. Even at this point, the attractive blonde woman was still finding the whole situation as a total farce all because she had called out the Queen of Hearts and now that brute was now putting Alice on trial for just speaking her mind.

"And I thought college campuses couldn't handle opinions," Alice thought darkly to herself as she was led into the dock with many eyes from all around staring at her. "Now I take that all back, God I can't believe I'm saying that..."

There was a feeling that something about this crowd felt fake as she got the vibe that they didn't like the Queen but were here to make the whole thing look impressive and show that they had their Queen's full support. Sounding just like any mad dictator that Alice could think about throughout history and she did have to wonder where they had picked up this poor people from to take part in this.

What made Alice livider was the fact that they were so determined to have this trail over so q uickly that even now they still wouldn't let Alice try and sew up her ripped jeans which meant her teal underwear was on show. She had never felt humiliated in all her life and all of this was just

making her furious and so tempted to punch that good for nothing Queen of Hearts in the face. Granted that would mean certain death but she would deserve it in all fairness.

The blonde-haired girl glanced around hoped for something or someone who could help get her out of this situation. Only one certain mad man was on her mind.

"Bloody hell where is he?" Alice muttered q uietly to herself as she remembered the Cat telling her about his mad plan. Surely her fiancée wouldn't leave her like this? Some dirty thoughts involving him running in like a gallant knight and saving her from her doom and the other, more likely oddly enough, being that of his large cock came to mind but she quickly shook them off; this was not the time for that though she would given anything to be mounted rather than be here.

Up in front of Alice was where the judge sat, though much to her dismay to show how stupid this trial was going to be, the Queen was going to act as the judge. If that didn't show how much of a kangaroo court this was going to be then what was Alice to do? Come to think of it made most kangaroo courts look good!

Just then the sound of a bugle was heard as Tobias ran through the room and up on to the pedestal next to the Queen. Once he got there, he cleared his throat and began to talk to the awaiting crowd. "Your royal majesty, members of the jury and loyal subjects, we will now begin the trial of Alice Bingsly."

"Kingsley!" Alice corrected in a hush tone. Bad enough this was happening to her, but they could not get her name right...? Still, she did find something weirdly fitting about her surname she never thought about before.

Kingsley. Sounds like 'king' as in Hatter's claim and of the possible future that might happen for the both of them if Alice didn't lose her head. Still, she didn't know if this was just coincidence or fate was really anyone's game, she just wanted to get out of here.

It was then Alice looked over at who made up the jury and was q uite amazed to see it made up of all the strange individuals she had met in Wonderland with them being Bill the Lizard, Tweedledum and Tweedledee, the Cheshire Cat (as he had said earlier) and for some reason there was the doorknob she first met when trying to get into Wonderland. The doorknob was lying on it's side and how they had gotten him was a mystery to Alice, but then again she didn't know what to think anymore.

Were they going to try and save her? She had no idea if that was the case of just there to watch what was nothing more than a show trial. Then again even if they were trying to help her in anyway they could, everything all seemed to be stacked against and conspire against poor Alice.

Alice though had many q uestions as to how the Queen was able to gather those certain characters in such a short time, then again, she remembered this was Wonderland and the one must always expect the strangest things.

As she thought about this, Tobias began to read a long list of paper. "The prisoner is charged with accusing her majesty, the Queen of Hearts, over a game of croquet with calls of slander, opinions, potential for violence and—"

"Just get to the witnesses, stupid!" The Queen snapped; Alice was speechless at how way out of proportion the whole thing was being expanded on.

The Rabbit mumbled nervously. "Um, now we move onto the main witness to give us the most unbiased information."

"Me!" The Queen cried and Alice face palmed. Poor rabbit looked like he did not want to be here.

For some reason it reminded Alice of a scene in the BBC comedy show 'Blackadder' that had such a one-sided courtroom scene. Come to think of it, she wouldn't mind having a binge watch of it sometime or somehow...

With the gathered audience awaiting with bated breath to hear the 'evidence', the Queen walked over down to the witness box and began looking greatly confident and started pointing angrily at Alice. "She called me horrible, ugly and a brute... lies about my character!"

Alice groaned; to say this was laughably one sided

would be an understatement. The crowd all made poor fake sounds of shock and despair. They did sound like they did not want to be there according to what Alice suspected The Queen then turned her gaze at the jury, who were fearful of her and Alice felt that they wanted to go home.

"What is the verdict?!" The Queen boomed. "And make it the choice I want!"

One of the shaken and scared jury, Bill, spoke for them. "W-we of t-the jury s-say...g-guilty."

"Sorry about all this dear Alice," the Cheshire Cat sighed sadly to the blonde girl. For once that huge smile on his face was gone which really did show that the poor cat meant it. So much for any help there.

The Queen beamed at the verdict she wanted. "Thank you, my dears," then she grinned menacingly at Alice. "Now with that statement...OFF WITH HER HEAD!"

Mock cheering followed with Tobias looking q uite pissed off (the black eye still troubling him) and muttered loudly claiming he wasn't getting paid enough to do this sort of thing and even insulted Alice briefly muttering why she had decided to come down to Wonderland in the first place, even though it was his fault it he knew it or not.

Despite this insult from the rabbit, Alice felt bad that here all animals could be underpaid and how horrible their lives must have been under the mad Queen's rule. The scary thought was how many more might be suffering out here in Wonderland that Alice did not see. One thing was certain if she were to ever get out of here, all animals would no longer be treated with cruelty but with kindness.

Alice was once again led away from the courtroom by the two card soldiers to a courtyard outside and it was here Alice was now fearful for her life as she saw the block she would have to rest her head on for the horrible end for her would happen. She looked around frantically trying to find something, anything, that could help her. In the crowd, she did think she saw a flash of red, but it was nothing.

Where was Hatter? Was this how she was going to end her curious yet horny life by being beheaded by an overgrown child who she called out on her horrible acts to animals? Only Alice could get into something like this and she started to see her life going past her eyes from his childhood, teenage years and of course falling down the rabbit hole and her new life in Wonderland in which she had hoped she'd live out the rest of her days out here in comfort and enjoyment. It was true Alice decided; people could never have nice things.

The crowd made up of card soldiers, animals and other strange Wonderland creatures were all there looking on and exactly where they had come from was a mystery to Alice, that was unless they were forced to watch. There were many animals she could recognise yet strangely enough that giant birdcage bird was nowhere to be seen. Maybe even the Queen of Hearts could not stand it, though Alice would have rather been that bird's meal again than having her head cut off.

Finally, Alice was forced to kneel by the block and her head being placed down. Behind her was one card soldier holding a bloody axe and glancing over to a balcony was the Queen of Hearts grinning at the spectacle about to unfold.

"Before you meet your end," the Queen suddenly said. "I'll be generous by giving you the chance to say your final words, any in mind?"

Oh, Alice had many to say to her, all of with involving every curse word in the English language and this wasn't including the fact that given how furious she was mainly that being bent over with her jeans stilled ripped meant that her fat ass and teal underwear were on show to many made her feel exposed.

Nonetheless Alice did have one thing to say to the Queen. "Off with your head you fat bitch!"
Alice said it with such venom that the crowd gasped, and the Queen went red in the face with anger, looking like she would explode with anger in which Alice hoped that would be the case, alas...

"OFF WITH HER HEAD, NOW!"

Alice shut her eyes and expected the end to befall on her. Instead, there was a scream, the sound of metal clashing and a certain male voice crying, "Alice!"

The said girl opened her eyes and there with a long sword with his sword pushing back the axe from getting near Alice's neck was a certain handsome man in red with a funny looking hat. no prizes as to guessing who it was. She did not care the logics how he could get a sword in there or how he got here or what had he been doing all this time; she was simply happy that he was here to save her.

Hatter leapt forward to disarm the solider with the axe, pushing him off the platform and into the crowd and this caused the crowd to panic with the Queen looking like she was going to burst with fury. Then in all the madness from archways leading into the courtyard were a certain Hare and Dodo, both with swords of their own. Hatter's army of Albert and Fredrick.

Alice couldn't believe it, Hatter's small army was actually here to save her! She looked up into the eyes of her hero and his eyes were filled with love and affection for her and it made Alice's heart skip a beat that he would do anything for her. Their tender moment though was shattered by the cry of that damn Queen.

"It's a damn Hightop!" Cried the Queen and began sniffing the air which which was filled with that husky smell from the Hatter and she remembered the smell Alive let off when she first met her and then she put two and two together. "You have been shagging that girl to be your queen! Your bloodline will not continue as long as I'm around to stop you once and for all!"

In the confusion, Hatter helped Alice up and she felt tempted to kiss him to show her gratitude but now was not the moment she told herself.

"You have to get out of the palace and into the mushroom field nearby!" Hatter instructed her. "What about you though?!" Alice demanded.
Hatter smiled. "Me and my buddies take care of the baddies. I have a throne to take back after all, plus I'm sure this is the time in which the people rise up to finally overthrow her. Look."

She looked over at the crowd and it only occurred to her that while the card soldiers were following orders from the Queen, everyone else seemed to be fighting back and some even cried out abuse to the Queen of Hearts. With that said, Alice did not say anything else and she made a hasty exit through a gap in the hedge with the scene behind her turning into a mutiny as what Hatter had hoped for.

The sight of the true king of Wonderland in that courtyard with is own (tiny) army caused many in the gathered crowed to take sides with him and troops clashed for control.

"Long live King Hatter!" Cried a voice.

"Down with the useless Queen of Hearts!" Another yelled out. "Wonderland will be free!" Roared another.
It was quite a battle though Alice did not look back

and just ran as far away as possible hoping that she would live another day as would her hopefully soon-to-be husband. For a so-called day out to take back the throne, it had all been a bit of a farce to be honest which had begun with a drugs moment, a game of croquet, a trial and planned execution. Then again, only in Wonderland could this only happen in and Alice should really known this by now.

Meanwhile back in the courtyard as the battled raged on, the Queen of Hearts was horrified that her reign looked doomed, but there was always one backup plan to catch Alice and Hatter which would finally end Alice and the Hightop clan once and for all.

"Send in the Jabberwocky to catch the girl!" The Queen cried out and Hatter only knew of the horrors that was the Queen of Hearts' favourite pet.

As the battled the forces of the Queen of Hearts, he only hoped that Alice would be safe. After taking done one enemy, he ran out of the place and followed Alice on the trail she had gone on with the Queen ordering those still loyal troops she had to follow Hatter.

What was to happen next though was one final trial of a different kind and one that might change the very future of Wonderland forever...that is if Alice stopped to play with herself yet again.
Though little did Alice realised that her biggest threat would soon be here...

CHAPTER 10
THE JABBERWOCKY

Chapter Summary: *After escaping from the Queen of Hearts, Alice encounters a truly scary creature that might make a meal out of Alice and all of Wonderland's last hopes...*

Alice did not know how long she had been running for. Though however long it might have been, her lungs felt like they were going to burst and what was worse was that she had no idea where she was. She eventually stopped running and she looked up to see that she was surrounded by large mushrooms that towered over her and decided then that with no noise of anyone or anything nearby, she decided to catch her breath by sitting on a smaller mushroom that thankfully did not sink under her fat ass.

While she was relieved at being safe at this moment from the Queen of Hearts, there was something unsettling about how quiet it was, too q uiet in fact. The sounds of animal life in the area was gone and that was something Alice had always heard in

Wonderland wherever she went so without hearing it was somewhat out of place, however her mind was preoccupied with a somewhat more pressing concern. One that after standing up again she rubbed her hand over her butt feeling that certain rip on her.

"Can't believe these jeans have to rip at a time like this of all days!" Alice bemoaned as she felt the rip that exposed her teal underwear to anyone who could see. "I hope Hatter is ok...once he has become king, will he still have time to fix my jeans? Of course, silly, Hatter can do that. Those wonderful hands of his can do anything..."

She knew it was foolish thought that Hatter would do that right now when he had more important things to worry about other than fixing her jeans, though just thinking about him made her feel better. Hatter was her knight in shining armour that was going to please her, and she began getting wet again as she started playing with herself yet again by rubbing her fingers on her ass through the ripped seam of her jeans.

There didn't seemed to be a day in the life of Alice at which she didn't stop once to play with herself which would have made her look crazy where she had come from before but in this mad world however, it was perhaps just part of life and more evidence to prove why Alice was perhaps well suited to live out in Wonderland.

Had she been paying attention; she would have heard the loud footsteps of something that was getting louder the more she played with herself and it was as the ground started to vibrate with each thud that Alice finally stopped, sticky fingers and all, and looked around trying to see where the sound was coming from.

If she had given herself more time to escape and not play with herself, she would not have had the chance to encounter perhaps the scariest looking creature she had ever come across that she couldn't even scream out of terror.

What stood there in front of her and gazed down at her was a large dragon like creature as big as a house with thick, brown scales with a tint of red markings, huge orange eyes as big as dinner plates and a large mouth filled with rows of sharp teeth that could likely chew through brick like butter.

The large creature Alice swore seemed to have a look of disgust, more likely due to the fact that the creature had seen Alice having, for lack of a better phrase, enjoying her private time which in all fairness might not had been the most unreasonable reaction.

Alice was about to run away but was stopped by the creature's thick tree trunk like tail and much to her surprise, it started speaking to her.

"Found you at last," the dragon spoke in a booming

voice. "You must be Alice Kingsley am I right?"

"Well...y-yes," Alice uttered, feeling scared about what lay in store for her. "Who are you and what do you want?"

The giant monster chuckled. "Apologies for my lack of manners, you can call me the Jabberwocky. So thus, we are now no longer strangers my dear. As for what I want? Simple really...a friend."

His relaxing tone, almost like some ASMR video one would find on the internet, made Alice feel more at ease and she dropped her guard. "Uh, well then, pleasure to meet you Mr...Jabberwocky. I must confess I don't think this is the best time to chat, but I must simply...wait, what did you ask for?"

"As I just mentioned, a friend," the Jabberwocky repeated and showed a toothy grin that he had this girl's attention.

The blonde girl gave the Jabberwocky a confused stare and pulled back a strand of her hair away from her face. "A friend? You mean me? Why? Is there no one else out here?"

"Haven't you noticed? It's lonely out here and there's no one else to speak to," the Jabberwocky answered as he motioned with his claw hand at the surrounding area around them.

Suddenly Alice's eyes widened as she remembered what Hatter had said about the Jabberwocky and what he had done to his family. How could she foolish to forget something so important so easily like that? "Wait! You are the monster that killed the Hightops!"

The Jabberwocky scoffed. "Heaven's sake are we going to bring that up? How would you know that is the truth as to why they are all gone?"

Alice was nearly caught off by his words but kept her ground. "I... Hatter told me what you have done! You're a monster!"

"Are you sure he was telling the truth?" The Jabberwocky inq uired, his head lowering down in which so that his large face was a few feet in front of her. "However, do I sense that there is something about Hatter you aren't telling me?"

A long silence followed and when the monster mentioned Hatter, she seemed to relax and Alice looked down at the engagement ring she had on and smiled. "Well, of course. Hatter asked me to marry him and become his q ueen. I have chosen to stay in Wonderland." She then muttered quietly to herself in which she added with, "especially if it means more of that magnificent cock."

Typical silly Alice no less...

The Jabberwocky seemed surprised and somewhat digusted by the fact that Alice would blurt out about Hatter's private parts in the open. "But you aren't of Wonderland and risk being trapped this world forever and never returning to your own?"

"I never felt I belonged in my own world," Alice admitted truthfully. "I feel like I belong here, such a curious and wonderful place in which I have no intention of leaving, even if it means I'm trapped here forever."

Alice felt a wave of excitement at the prospect of being 'trapped' in Wonderland, no doubt her parents would've freaked out if they knew or even cared what had happened to her and her sexual romps that they had tried to discourage her to do during her early adulthood. She loved to rebel against her upper middle-class upbringing and the Jabberwocky seemed to sense of how committed Alice was to her cause. Perfect for what he had planned for her.

"My dear, do you really want to stay in Wonderland forever?"

"More than I have ever been sure, and life will be better once that horrible Queen of Hearts is gone!" Alice replied with confidence, though this only gave the Jabberwocky the confidence to act out his orders, especially after her words terrible about the Queen.

"Very well then, Alice. I can help you stay in Wonderland and achieve your dreams if you follow my advice."

"Oh? What would that be?"

The Jabberwocky held back a chuckle, he knew she had got her where he wanted and had easily hooked her as if he was fishing. "First thing to say, I want you to look into my eyes."

"Look? What do you mean by—Oh!" Alice was suddenly finding her vision growing fuzzy as the last thing she remembered was the Jabberwocky's orange eyes began to glow a pale orange and before long she felt her body feeling tingly and exciting.

The large brown monster chuckled loudly seeing how Alice, now her blue eyes replaced with glowing orange eyes, had fallen easily to his villainous charms. To easy as a matter of fact. "That's right Alice, look into my eyes and all your troubles will wash away. Yes dear, Alice. Just relax..."

With a loud 'ping' sound in her head, Alice was now under the Jabberwocky's control and she stood there with her arms by her side and had a silly grin stuck on her face. "Oh goodness," Alice moaned. "This feels so good. Oh, I feel dizzy."

The Jabberwocky laughed at seeing how easy this girl

had been so easily hypnotized, not to mention how tasty this girl looked with her slender body, tasty looking bottom and long golden blonde hair, he secretly couldn't really blame Hatter for having an eye on this girl and likely nailing her to his bed. Alas that was not important, he had to carry out his task from Queen of Hearts had set out for him.

Devour Alice and hopefully do the same with Hatter and end the Hightop line once and for all to keep the Queen of Hearts as ruler of Wonderland.

However, with Alice in her current hypnotised state and disappointed in a way how easy she had been to fall to his charms, he decided to have a bit of fun with Alice as he could do anything with her. "Now my delicious, Alice...I want you to dance for me."

The blonde girl moaned slightly as she was feeling herself get wet again and slurred as she tried to speak. "But...I don't know how to...dance..."

"Just listen to my words," The Jabberwocky ordered, his tone relaxing her senses. "Now, slowly start swaying for me."

"Y-yes, master," Alice replied and started doing what the Jabberwocky ordered.

"Ah! Very good!" The Jabberwocky congratulated her as he enjoyed her swaying her hips from side to side. "Now then, start swaying your hips and show me that large rear end of yours. The world deserves to see such a stunning girl like yourself display to the world like that."

Alice followed orders and began to dance in a sexy manner that she would never had done before but in her current state, she slowly turned round to show the Jabberwocky her fat ass by slowly shaking it for him and acting as if she were a belly dancer and despite the fact she didn't know how to dance, the hypnotised state was helping her to the point as one just walking in on the scene would had thought Alice had been doing those sort of dances for years.

The Jabberwocky laughed as he loved the sight of this girl dancing for him and this was especially upon seeing her fat bottom and noticing the rip on the back of her jeans that revealed her now very wet teal underwear and not to mention that he was rather enjoying this private show that no one else could have the pleasure of seeing. Alice in her brainless state had no idea what she was doing as she danced in a sexual manner; however, she was greatly enjoying this feeling nonetheless as she rubbed her hands over her breasts, crotch and ass while moaning softly.

As much as the Jabberwocky would have loved to have watched this all day, he had seen enough and decided to finish his task before he had other ideas. "Very good my sexy slave! Now you can stop." Alice stopped dancing and looked up into the Jabberwocky's eyes. "Would you like to go on another adventure that is beyond your wildest imagination?"

"Mmm, oh yes...I love this feeling!" Alice cried out with her voice sounding like she was about to have an orgasm.

"Then prepared for an adventure you'll never return from," the Jabberwocky replied with a chuckle and began to coil his long thick tail around Alice. His scales sent little electric shocks throughout Alice's body and by the time the coils had wrapped round her breasts, Alice was moaning in mad pleasure at feeling tightly coiled up and finally she let out an orgasm.

"My, my. Someone must have a fetish for being in tight places," the Jabberwocky chuckled and slowly raised Alice off the ground and flicked his snake like tongue out to taste her. "Mmm, you taste delicious.

That smooth skin and that enormous bottom of yours will fill me up nicely for a whole week. Alas, we have to end it like this sadly, prepare for your final adventure, Alice."

With that, he opened his huge mouth began to eat a hypnotized Alice. Even though she didn't know about the deadly situation she was in, this weird feeling being inside the mouth was causing her to ejaculate like crazy and her nectar was now acting like a lubrication to swallow her whole, something that the Jabberwocky was probably needing for as he unravelled his tail, he found that one half of Alice would not go in. Yes, her fat ass had probably saved her to hopefully not end up in a similar situation like the birdcage bird. Frustrated, the Jabberwocky raised his head upwards to help him finally get all of Alice's body into his mouth which after he managed to get her large ass inside the mouth, her legs were slurped up like strands of spaghetti.

All trace of Alice had gone and with a final swallow, a bulge of what was once Alice could be seen slowly making its way down the long serpent like neck. The Jabberwocky let out a booming laugh at his triumph and at such a tasty meal and even yells of pleasure could be heard coming from inside the long neck much to the giant monster's amusement.

"Foolish girl, you should've not let your curiosity get the better of you. But do not worry, you'll be with Hatter Hightop if he appears soon. Now then, where is that clown of a man?"

Ironically just as he said that the Mad Hatter was now q uite literally mad, (madder than usual no less and not in the best way one will add) came running in roaring holding his sword while the Queen of Hearts and her troops were chasing him. Seeing that his beloved Alice was on the verge of entering the stomach as she went further down the neck, Hatter decided to end this nightmare for Wonderland for good.

The Jabberwocky prepared his hypnotised glowing eyes on Hatter however the sight of seeing Alice going down the giant monster's throat was enough fuel for him to go in for the kill and put down the monster once and for all. Hatter came rushing in so fast that the Jabberwocky didn't have time to react as before he knew it, he felt a rush of pain on the base of his neck as Hatter began lashing at it with the sword and blood began to show but Hatter had to be q uick as he saw the bulge of Alice was getting close towards the main body of the beast in which once Alice reached the stomach, she would be digested q uickly much like the rest of Hatter's family before her.

No way was he going to let another person he cared about suffer from the Jabberwocky, especially if it was an incredible woman like Alice who even though he had only known for a few days knew that she was his soulmate.

The giant dragon creature attempted to try and catch Hatter in its mouth, but the brunette man managed to avoid capture by rolling over to the other side of the Jabberwocky and then struck several more blows at the Jabberwocky in which the wound on the neck became more open, deep and bloody. It was only a matter of time surely now.

Watching this scene as she arrived, the Queen of Hearts could only look on with horror at the sight of her prized animal was on the verge of death and with that...her power too of controlling Wonderland.

"Quick! Stop him!" She ordered her loyal troops who all as ordered went rushing into to try and stop Hatter.

However, with Hatter, with one final slash of his now bloodied sword and the huge head of the Jabberwocky trying to get Hatter in his mouth, the sword went right through the neck in which blood and slime went pouring out and like a large timber tree, the long serpent neck of the Jabberwocky went falling to the ground with a crash which made the ground shake with force.

As soon as the neck hit the ground, the card soldiers all stopped dead in their tracks and the Queen of Hearts' eyes widened at the sight of her prized pet decapitated and only knew what this only meant for.

Hatter grinned at the shocked Queen and had one joke he could not help but speak out. "Look at that, seems he lost his head, like with all of those you beheaded."

"How dare you!" The Queen cried out. "Guards! Off with his head!"

But they did not move. Her worst fears had come true and this did not go unnoticed by Hatter who now knew where the real power now lay.

"Guards, control her!" Hatter ordered and those guards which were under the Queen's control all turned round to face her with contempt looks and marched towards her and she backed off in fear fearing what was about to happen. The tables had finally turned.

"No...No! Stop them!" She cried out but it was all too late.

"Your reign of terror is over," Hatter stated. "No more will Wonderland suffer under your brutal rule and peace will finally reign over the land."

At this point, some of the guards leapt in and grabbed the Queen by her arms and she cried out in anger as she tried to get out of their grasp. "You traitorous bastards!"

"No point trying to argue with them," Hatter said drily. "It's over."

The Queen of Hearts now looked for the first time in her life to be in fear. Fear about after all what she done to those who had not followed her rule was about to fall upon her. "No...w...what are you planning to...?"

Hatter grinned and threw the sword to the ground. "Behead you? No way, I'm too kind for that. I have a better fate for you...guards...banish her away from Wonderland and make sure she never returns to these lands ever again!"

"NOOO! HOW COULD YOU!? IMPRUDENT HIGHTOP BASTARD!"

And thus while kicking and screaming, the guards dragged the evil Queen away into the distance and thus, on her way out off Wonderland and forever banished from these lands. As soon as she was gone and well out of sight, a silence fell upon the land and it felt like even Wonderland itself seemed to notice that change had happened and suddenly the sound of animal life returned.

However, Hatter had something more important to do as he rushed over to the base of the decapitated neck and there poking out from the base of it was the blonde hair of a certain girl that Hatter had risked his life to save. She had barely avoided from reaching the stomach.

"Alice! Are you alright?" Hatter cried out as he carefully dragged the slimy yet alive body of Alice out from her fleshy cocoon. Despite all soaked from head to toe in saliva from the Jabberwocky, she was breathing and the effects of her hypnotised state were starting to die off. It didn't matter that she was covered in slime, she was still the most beautiful woman he had ever seen in his life and this only made him want her to become his Queen even more so...something that was now going to happen with the evil Queen of Hearts banished.

"Ugh, my head," Alice slurred as she slowly sat up rubbing her head and then groaned in disgust at seeing the slime all over her which indicated that she was no longer under the monster's influence. "W...what happened...Hatter?"

She stared up at her soulmate and despite being covered in gunk, she pulled down Hatter to smother him in a fiery kiss to show her gratitude that he was safe. After they kissed, the brunette male pulled back and smiled at her.

"Well...that's one-way of saying thanks," Hatter grinned.

"Hatter, what happened? What happened to me?" Alice asked looking down at herself.

"You won't like this," Hatter replied. "Let's just say that things might have not gone well for all of us..."

He then explained what had happened and how she had been almost a tasty meal for the Jabberwocky. By the time he had told Alice this, the blonde woman was furious about being caught out like that and so stood up quickly and kicked the lifeless body of the huge dragon like beast.

"That rotten bastard!" Alice yelled. "How could I let myself get into that situation?! God, I need a wash badly.

"You will my dear and much more," Hatter assured her as he slowly walked over to her to stand in front of her before wrapping his arms round her waist.

"What'd you mean?" Alice asked, though this only made Hatter roll his eyes.

"Silly girl, don't you know what it all means now that the Queen of Hearts is gone?"

Alice pondered for a moment though a suggestive expression from Hatter suddenly made everything in her click. "Oh...OH! You...when do we...?"

"Tomorrow," Hatter purred and kissed her softly. "Not only a wedding but a coronation. Wonderland will be ours to rule in peace."

"And I couldn't hope for anything better," Alice sighed and the two lovers rested their foreheads on each other and just stood there in silence thinking about how both their lives, and by all extension everyone else in Wonderland, were all about to change for the better. A new era in Wonderland was about to happen.

CHAPTER 11
A CORONATION AND WEDDING

Chapter Summary: It is finally for Alice and Hatter to tie the knot as well as begin their new lives as King and Queen of Wonderland...

When the news spread around Wonderland that the evil Queen of Hearts had been banished, there was much celebration and joy for much of the citizens of Wonderland for not just the fact that they would no longer living in fear from the mad queen, but rather that their true king would regain the throne and peace would return to Wonderland...or peaceful in Wonderland terms. To add more to this wonderful news was that not only would Hatter be getting a coronation to become King of Wonderland, but it would also act as a wedding for it was here that he would marry Alice Kingsley who in turn was to become Queen of Wonderland.

Speaking of which, the day following the defeat of the Queen of Hearts, Alice was left amazed at the madcap preparations were all being made in just as Hatter had said to Alice, they would be married the following day and thus the courtyard in the palace was all decked out in bunting for what was to be a big day for Wonderland. How in the world they had been able to pull all of this off in such a short time was something of a mystery to Alice, then again she assumed that given how much of the citizens of Wonderland hated the Queen of Hearts, they must had been secretly planning for this to happen. Sounds crazy but then again this was Wonderland.

It was stranger, actually no, strange was now considered normal, that even within the last twenty-four hours that there was even time for a wedding dress for Alice to be ready for her and that night in the palace, the first that Alice had not been with Hatter, had tried it on to see how it looked and Alice was amazed at what her wedding dress was like. It was white but had red trim across it and it had a slim fit to it in which hugged Alice's curves nicely all making her look like a Disney princess, though it did of course made her bottom look bigger than it already was. Or had her rear gotten larger since she had many of Hatter's cakes? Either way, she really could not tell.

That all said as she looked at herself in the mirror she did feel beautiful and despite it being such a big occasion in Wonderland, it would only struck Alice in the following morning that it was to be her wedding day and it was a bizarre feeling that after living a life in which she never thought a man would love her for what she was, let alone have a wedding, but then again here she was about to marry not only the man of her dreams but also become a q ueen for this crazy yet wonderful land. How was life to get better than this?

The morning itself, a bright sunny day as it always seemed to be in Wonderland, was q uite a relaxed one as Alice had been given breakfast in bed which she wolfed down without much thought and got herself fitted up into her dress in what she hoped would be trouble free and thankfully there was no problem when she slipped on the dress. Though she was happy about her wedding, there was a small part in her that did wish her parents could be here in someway despite all the grievances she had about them. Part of her did like the idea of her Dad walking down the aisle as what most Dads would have wanted...then she shook her head at the thought.

No way her parents would approve of her actions here mainly at the fact Alice had only known Hatter for a few days before agreeing to marry him and with the many trials and tribulations Alice had gotten herself involved with, she knew that hearing all of this would have freaked her parents out and would have ordered not to go through with this.

"Screw them," Alice muttered to herself.

Wonderland was now her home and no one, not even her parents were ever going to change her mind otherwise. Boy, how she would have loved to have seen their reactions about where their daughter had ended up and how well she had done for herself. Nothing better than sticking it right up to those who doubt you.

Speaking though of absent fathers, Alice though was to be taken down the aisle by Albert the Dodo which did seem like a good suggestion given how he had been one of the first Alice had met in Wonderland and had saved her from the birdcage bird as well as playing a part in helping to overthrow the Queen of Hearts; a suitable character no doubt.

As Alice was doing final adjustments to her dress in her bedroom, the door knocked.

"Come in!" Alice called out and in stepped in was Albert all dressed up smartly as what a humanoid

Dodo would look like if one could imagine it.

"My goodness my Queen you look stunning!" Albert complimented and Alice held back a blush. "Thank you, Albert. But I'm not the Queen."
"Not yet," Albert replied. "I'm sure you'll be a fairer queen than that other useless hag we had to suffer under."

The blonde bride paused at the thought of her new and most unlikely role that only a few days ago she would never had thought in her wildest drams that this would have happened, but here it was. "Albert, who is here for the wedding?"

"Nearly all of Wonderland if you ask me!" Albert noted. "There are also the other distance relative clans of our new King that have come to honour him."

"Hatter has relatives?" Alice asked curiously.

The Dodo nodded. "Oh, indeed. Despite what you might think, neither of them dared to challenge the mad q ueen for the throne because they felt Prince Hatter, or King Hatter I should say, should take it for himself and that's that you can say."

Alice nodded, she remembered the stories Hatter had told Alice when they were cuddled up in his bed as he had told her the different clans related to him that all bowed down to the Hightop line and that soon they'd all be bowing down to her by the end of the day. Then she thought about those nights cuddle close to him and her his touch made her feel all relaxed and turned on...

No, as much as she would've liked to fondle herself thinking about her future husband, now wasn't the time as she had a wedding to do and plus she would have more fun tonight...

"Albert, I think it's time to go," Alice announced as

she grabbed her bouq uet of flowers.

"Allow me to lead the way," Albert replied and linking her arm with his wing/arm, they both headed down towards the palace courtyard in which the wedding was to take place.

"Albert, just one more thing," Alice then piped up. "What's that?"
Alice paused before saying what she had to say. "Nothing much to say but...Thank you." The dodo was taking aback. "I'm sorry, what for?"
"For what you have done," Alice explained, "you helped me when I was in that birdcage bird and in helping Hatter. Nothing really much to say other than that."

Albert smiled. "Always a pleasure my dear."

Along the many corridors on the way there, many of those card soldiers who had once been loyal to the

Queen of Hearts were now all lined up by many of the walls in the palace and were standing
to attention to their new q ueen and Alice felt a giddiness of what power she will soon have over this land though she was wanting to use it for good causes.

By the time they reached the entrance to the courtyard, the wedding music began and many of the hundreds of guests there all stood up to acknowledge her arrival. It was a sunny day and Alice stared at the crowd as she walked down the aisle and soon saw familiar faces she had met on her travels such as Tweedledee and Tweedledum who were both crying; there's always one or two who cry at weddings.

There were also those animals she met on the beach that Albert was trying to dry off that Alice remembered but what took her eye was several human folks in the crowd that were dressed in matching royal outfits that were either in blue, green or yellow, yet all had black trousers for the men or skirts for the ladies and these were from the other clans that Hatter had talked about.

Speaking of matching sets, the male outfits all matched that of the Groom at the end of the aisle and the sight of the man dressed in red and black made Alice blush.

Seeing Hatter dressed in his royal attire with a row of medals on him, golden epaulettes and buttons and a sword on his side, Alice thought he looked very handsome and it was true that was something about a man dressed in uniform and Alice could not wait to get her hands on him after this wedding. Actually, during that walk down the aisle, just seeing him dressed up was starting to make her feel wet and she had to try and fight the urge not to show this in front of the many here. The one thing that was missing from Hatter was his large hat though Alice remembered that it was his crown and seeing it on a cushion by the priest, which turned out to be Bertie the once ex- caterpillar now butterfly, which she knew he would be crowned after the vows were done. It was strange to see him without his hat and his brunette hair was thick, curly and went down to his shoulders and Alice loved to run her fingers through Hatter's hair.

Once Alice was up by the alter beside Hatter, Albert let go of her and he rushed back to his chair in the front row and now the wedding could begin.

"Good day all," Bertie announced to the crowd, his tone sounding rather bored despite the grand occasion. "We are gathered here today for the wedding of Prince Hatter Hightop and Alice Kingsley and for their Coronation. Let us begin this."

Alice was confused; wasn't there supposed to be a bit in which the priest asked for the crowd to speak out if they did not think the couple should be married? Then again Alice put it down to different things in

Wonderland and she didn't care, she wanted to be married to her Hatter now.

"Prince Hatter Hightop," Bertie looked at the groom. "Do you take this woman to your wife and Queen of Wonderland?"

"I do," Hatter replied and smiled at his soulmate.

Bertie now looked over at Alice. "And do you, Alice Kingsley, take this man to your husband and King of Wonderland?"

"I do, always," Alice answered happily.

"Very well, now for the rings," Bertie called out, his tone sounding more bored and out from the crowd came Tobias who handed over a purple cushion with two matching gold rings on them.

As Alice and Hatter slipped on each other rings on,

the bride couldn't help but have a glance over the rabbit who if not for him, she would never had ended up down that rabbit hole and start a new life in this world. Once the rings were on, the couple stared at each other desperate to grabbed each other.

"I now pronounce you man and wife," Bertie announced, "you may now—"

But he didn't, much to his annoyance, get to finish the speech as both Alice and Hatter grabbed each other close and gave each other a hot, steamy kiss in front of the crowd. It was their first kiss as a married couple and they felt that their two souls seemed to join as one.

The crowd cheered, whooped and some cried at the happy scene and after the married couple pulled away, Hatter looked over at the grumpy butterfly and knew that there was still one more yet important task to do.

Alice stepped back to allow Hatter to kneel as Bertie prepared to place his hat, or rather crown, on him and after this was done and he stood up, Bertie then handed over a sceptre and orb for Hatter to hold and he turned towards the crowd who all stood to attention.

"From this day forward," Bertie announced to the crowd. "Now begins to reign of King Hatter of Wonderland. Long live the King!"

"LONG LIVE THE KING!" The crowd responded and erupted in cheers and thus, both Hatter and Alice were now not only husband and wife, but also the King and Queen of Wonderland.

Though the ceremony had been a short affair, being somewhat over in a blur for Alice, the aftermath party was, well, a mad affair in which everyone seemed to be having the time of their lives which might have been well as now they no longer lived in fear by were now overjoyed that their true King had returned and also a Queen who they felt would be a worthy wife for their newly crowned King.

During the dinner, Alice and Hatter went around many of the tables to greet the many guests who all spoke highly of the couple though as much as Alice enjoyed this, she did though want to get away to somewhere more...private.

It was then late in the evening in which much of the crowd were dancing to music being played by the band, many of them utterly plastered by the gallons of drink that had been consumed, that Hatter noticed his wife was looking rather bored by the main table and q uickly went over to see what was wrong.

"Are you alright my dear?" Hatter asked his wife as he walked up to her.

"Well of course," Alice replied, "though I will confess all of this has made me rather, tired." Her handsome husband smiled. "Not to worry by dear, we can head straight to bed if you like."

"But won't they notice we're missing?" Alice questioned, "it would be rather rude if we left so suddenly."

Hatter laughed. "Not at all my dear; that lot are going to be dancing for the whole night and won't notice we've gone."

"The whole night? Isn't that all a bit mad?" Alice inq uired. "We're all mad here, remember?"
"Oh yes...point taken. Can't believe I'd forget that"

Suddenly Alice was lifted in the air and Hatter now carrying her bridal style. "Ready for pleasure my dear Alice?" Hatter purred suggestively which made Alice shudder with excitement.

"Oh yes my darling husband," Alice purred in response, putting on a lot of emphasis on the last word there.

With that, King Hatter now carried away his blonde queen back into the palace in which the rest of everyone else were left oblivious to their sudden absence. After going up a few corridors, they ended up in what was now to be their bedroom and it was a grand room that felt lush with many tones of red and all of it felt as if it were fit for a King and Queen to sleep in, or rather, have lots of sex in it and and both Hatter and Alice were going to have a lot of that from now on.

Hatter gently lay his wife on the bed in which he began to undress herself much to Alice's excitement who had been looking forward to this all day.

"Ready for our first night as husband and wife?" Hatter asked with a grin.

"I'm already wet for you," Alice uttered intimately, her eyes showing much desire and want in them.

Hatter slowly removed his clothes until his was wearing just his black trousers and Alice licked her lips of seeing how well toned his body was. Alice in turn had also slipped off her wedding dress revealing just a frilly set of white panties and a bra, then when Hatter dropped his trousers and his large cock appeared, there was only going to be one thing where that was going to end up.

Like a mad hungry child for ice cream, Alice pounced forward to grab Hatter's manhood and began give him an almighty blowjob. Hatter groaned with delight as he felt the sensation of his wife's lips around his cock and she really was q uite amazing at it and truly deserved to be treated like gold, so good was the feeling that after about a minute, he felt it happening.

"Alice! I-I'm gonna...!"

He didn't get to finish as before long, he cummed his load into Alice's mouth who swallowed it hungrily. Then before long Alice positioned herself into a doggy position in which she removed her bra and panties off to show off his wonderful fat ass on display which was enough to keep Hatter t have a raging boner. He climbed onto the bed in which he spanked her ass cheeks and chuckled at hearing her moan and seeing the ass cheeks jiggle after the spank.

He then thrusted himself into his wife and she cried out in pleasure as she gripped the red pillows. "Oh God, HATTER!" Alice cried out, "Fill me up, PLEASE!"
"Always my wonderful q ueen," Hatter replied in a husky voice and only did what was needed to please his wife as before long Alice's own pussy was dripping from Hatter's seed and neither of them wanted this

incredible sex session to end, but eventually both would end up getting exhausted from it all and would finally fall asleep cuddling each other naked. With that said, their first night as a married couple would be one of utter passion, love and excitement in which was much better than what either of them could have hoped for though for the rest of Wonderland, a new era had begun.

CHAPTER 12

A CURIOUS NEW LIFE

Chapter Summary: One Month after their wedding and coronation, Alice reflects on her new life in Wonderland and for what the future might hold for her...

Once there was a 25-year-old attractive looking blonde girl called Alice Kingsley who despite coming off a well-off family and upbringing was never truly satisfied as she was deemed a social outcast due to her imaginative and weird outlook on life. She did her own thing throughout life until one day she just seemed to disappear and weirdly no one seemed to notice that she was gone and even more strangely all records of a girl called Alice Kingsley seem to vanish. Not only was it liked as if she never existed to begin with but also feeling like as if she had pretty much fallen off the face of the earth.

Ironically in many ways, the latter was the literal truth as what happened to Alice. The reason for suddenly disappearing? While relaxing in a field one sunny day, she saw a white rabbit in a waistcoat and followed it to a large rabbit hole in which she went through and suddenly fell downwards in a bottomless pit. Little did she know then was not only that the last time she would be seen by anyone in her world, but that Alice would find herself in a strange new world called Wonderland. A place that time there was radically different to how it was on Earth meaning that would make it impossible to return to return to her world at the same time when she left should she ever return somehow. However, despite this fact that she could never return given how it had become q uite clear that falling into Wonderland had been in many ways a one way trip, she couldn't be happier with life as Wonderland was a place she felt more alive and suited to than what had come before.

Following her fall down that rabbit hole and finding herself in Wonderland, Alice would end up going on a wild journey that often involved getting her fat bottom getting stuck, eating lots of cake, meeting many weird and strange creatures and characters, fall in love with a man known as Hatter Hightop, who wasn't really human and known by many as the Mad Hatter, who was none other than the lost king of Wonderland and in turn overthrow a horrible Queen of Hearts who had killed Hatter's family.

But above all and perhaps more important to Alice, lots and lots of sex with her new husband and soulmate, Hatter.

To say Alice had never done anything so outrageous and un-lady like as all of this would be an understatement. Following her fateful choice to remain in Wonderland, Alice would from then on become a permanent resident of Wonderland and life in this weird yet wonderful world would become better by all. You see, Alice Kingsley of Marchmont Edinburgh would be no more, instead she would become Queen Alice Hightop of Wonderland after marrying Hatter Hightop who had been crowned

King of Wonderland following the successful overthrow of the Queen of Hearts. That was one way to stick it to her socially climbing obsessed parents who Alice had no doubt would had a fit in they found out what she had gotten herself into or perhaps being extremely jealous that Alice had ended in a high class positing that they would likely never get in their lifetime. Nothing better than to stick it up to them according to Alice, though at the same time she did wondered given how even before falling into Wonderland she and her parents were starting to drift apart so either way they would split one way or the other.

For the rest of the people of Wonderland in the wake of the Queen of Hearts' forced removal in which saw her banished from Wonderland, Hatter would take the throne becoming the true king of Wonderland in a joint Coronation and wedding ceremony that seemed all rather intimate yet crazy which in a way was only fitting for someone known as the Mad

Hatter. Nonetheless the population of Wonderland all took their new king and q ueen to heart and had high hopes that they would be more kinder rulers than what either had been used to for so many years.

Alice would find this funny, as it was like a Disney princess movie in which the princess marries the boy after just a few days which despite Alice always finding this stupid was exactly what had happened here in which Alice and Hatter had only known each other for barely over a week by the time they wedded, yet in Wonderland, a rational thought was never really something that applied here. Regardless though and how hypocritical she might had been of thinking about the Disney connection, Alice was happy to have more of Hatter's tasty cock inside of her which seemed to a great plus in her new married life as Queen of Wonderland.

It wasn't just new rulers that Wonderland was experiencing as following the coronation, Hatter had been studying the world in which Alice came from and had made the choice to introduce democracy to Wonderland in which Hatter and Alice would become a constitutional monarch. It would make things less demanding for the young royal couple, though it was fair to say some of the choices to govern Wonderland were bizarre to say the least. Then again should've Alice been surprised by this by now?

For example, the Prime Minster would be Hatter's friend Fredrick, Albert would become Minster of Finance and Tobias would end up as Secretary of State. It was though as one looked at it as something akin to nepotism due to the fact that Hatter knew all of them as close friends however to give them all credit they all did their jobs very well and honestly it was hard to think of anyone around here of who might be more suited to run Wonderland than them.

At last with all that had happened, in conclusion, Alice was genuinely happier than she'd ever been in her life and nothing could get any better than this as she felt her life now had a purpose.

It was now just over a month since Hatter and Alice had become king and q ueen and they were at that moment sitting on their thrones (which were their comfortable shiny red leather chairs from Hatter's garden) while in the throne room greeting their subjects while holding each other's hands being that they sat close to each other. They were pretty much in love as everyone could see though while Alice would have been wearing a royal blue dress due to being Queen of Wonderland (one that Alice had seen on that portrait on her fall down the rabbit hole), she was instead dressed in her usual attire of tight jeans, blue camisole and short sleeved white blouse which was all very un-royal like things to wear, but she was planning to explore more of Wonderland and needed to be dressed in something a little bit more comfortable. She wouldn't want to ruin her lovely dress anyway.

As the last of their subjects left the room, as well as their card soldiers leaving just the two of them in the room, the blonde-haired girl smiled at her husband then looked over at a long table on the other side of the room which had, to no one's surprise, lots of cake that was just begging it seemed to be eaten. No need to guess as what might happen next "Something seems to have you smiling," Hatter noted.

"You of course silly," Alice chuckled. "I just feel so...alive and complete."

Hatter then laughed as Alice got up and rushed over towards a large plate of pink cake she had been eying up to eat for a while now due to them meeting their subjects and before one could say anything, she began to devour the cake in a very un-q ueen like way.

For some reason, Hatter seeing this behaviour, as

well as her tight jeans (repaired now after she accidentally ripped them) showed her curves nicely being bent showing her large fat ass on display and this only seemed to turn King Hatter on as he developed a bulge in his trousers. Not a very king like thing to do, then again, he was mad as one already knew and his feelings for the blonde there was so strong that he found himself doing the one thing he could only do. He unzipped his black trosusers, pulled down his boxers and began stroking his rock hard cock.

In typical Alice fashion, it didn't take long for her to finish the cake in which she moaned in pleasure and as she turned round, she was amused seeing that now, Hatter had pulled his trousers down and had been jerking off to Alice during that time in which he moaned softly and his eyes were rolling into the back of his head.

"Goodness! I must be that good for you to do that,"

Alice laughed. "But that reminds me, a Queen does need her dessert and I feel you have much of what I want."

"After eating all that cake? Good heavens!" Hatter slurred as he found himself getting turned out like crazy.

With that, Alice skipped over towards Hatter, got on her knees and began to give King Hatter a blowjob he wouldn't forget. Hatter groaned in pleasure and Alice in turn loved how fuzzy the fuzzy brown hair around his manhood felt. With them being both sexual charged at this point, it didn't take long for them to reach their climaxes with Hatter groaning as his cum spluttered in Alice's mouth and she loved it whenever she had her husband's seed in her mouth.

"Doesn't take long for things to happy my delicious q ueen," Hatter said in a husky tone as she sat back on his throne breathing heavily as his exposed cock was now dripping from the romp just now.

"Oh, indeed my handsome king," Alice replied as she enjoyed the taste. "However, even though I love my cake, I've felt a weird craving for tuna and ice cream, curious I must say."

The brunette king did not think much of it, though suspected that she might be pregnant though he might be thinking too much into. With that though, he pulled Alice on his lap in which she playfully wriggled on Hatter's cock which was still rock solid in which the texture of her jeans and just how plush her fat bottom was to him all helped him find this all very sexy. "All seriousness though...I don't what I'd do without you. Without you I may have not only found my soulmate, but also help me retake the throne. I love you so much dear Alice."

Alice was greatly touched by this and placed a soft kiss on his lips. "Oh Hatter, it should be me thanking you as in my world I never fit in there, but here is where my life truly begins and I'm happy to spend the rest of my life with you. I love you too my Hatter Hightop."

The two of the leaned close and nuzzled noses together before Hatter thought of something. "My dear, why is a raven like a writing desk?"

Alice raised an eyebrow. "Well I...I haven't the slightest idea."

"Neither do I," Hatter chuckled at his random riddle before letting Alice sit up by giving her a playful spank on her bottom. Something Alice hated before she ended up in Wonderland but now loved it whenever Hatter did it. Those wonderful hands of his could do anything good and that included playful spanks.

"If you excuse me," Alice then announced. "I must go

out and explore, I feel that there are many more curious things to discover in Wonderland."

"Well, it is your kingdom too after all," Hatter added. "You can do whatever you want though be careful with the many strange creatures out there. "

The queen smiled though knew that Hatter had a good point to be on the lookout. It was always good to be a ruler, so much fun. "I hope you'll be alright while I'm gone, I shouldn't be that long."

"Be back for tea," Hatter instructed. "I must get many forums done and meet with my minsters, hopefully they won't being pulling of anything stupid. Take care my dear."

"Have a great day at work dear," Alice replied and with that said, the new q ueen of Wonderland set up on a new adventure in what was now her kingdom. Quite a leap from what she had only owned before was some small flat.

One thing she had noticed about the palace was that the interior was very much like Hatter's cottage in which it had many bookcases lining the walls, the beige walls were also giving off a warm feeling and in truth it was like everything Hatter had in that cottage had been brought here to the palace and Alice did like this as it gave a very homely feel which considering this was now her permanent stay of residence was not all that surprising.

Whenever she went past guards, they always bowed and said 'your majesty' to her and Alice did love how she felt in control. She found herself eventually walking in the garden in which she had played that game of croq uet with the former queen. One horrible thing that had happened before that Alice hated was that had been used cruelly for the games by the evil Queen of Hearts, thankfully they were now all free and mingling around the garden like nothing had even happened to them. No animal was to be cruelly treated in her kingdom and there had a been a few times in which many grateful animals who could talk couldn't thank her enough for her actions.

Walking down the path leading outside the castle grounds, a row of soldiers on either side stood for attention and Alice smiled seeing how she could almost do anything and they would do her very command. Eventually she was on her way out of the castle grounds and into a thick woodland that had tangerine trees and giant mushrooms towering over her.

She knew she had to be careful in remembering her husband's words due to some of the wildlife that was big enough to eat her, she had already come across two attempts on her life that might have seen her end, however as she sat on a smaller mushroom and giggled how it formed nicely around her ass due to how soft it was, she began to think of the future.

She knew that even if she wanted to go back to her world, the timeline between both Wonderland and her world were so out of sync that it was impossible to get back to where she started and that if she ever did return somehow, it would seemed like as if she had never existed there to begin with.

As horrible as this might have sounded for someone's life to be cleared from Earth, Alice didn't care, this was her Wonderland, and she couldn't be better-off for it. So happy was she that she began to play with herself yet again and fantasizing of what the future held for her. There were more lands outside Wonderland to explore and her curious nature seemed to tempt her to find out what was out there.

After she finished playing with herself and getting her silky teal underwear wet, she headed off to find what else was there to be found in Wonderland and beyond. She had to hide though behind a mushroom stalk as she saw that large birdcage bird padding along looking for something to eat.

Something that Alice hoped wouldn't be her again. That all being said, she strangely found the idea of being eaten weirdly sexy, had she gained some kind of fetish out here? Then again, weird things usually turned Alice on and in many regards one could see how she seemed to have fitted in this strange world like a duck to water.

As she carried on walking down a pink path and looking around her, Alice was truly in Wonderland. A Wonderland filled with adventure, weirdness, sex, cake, and more sex to follow. What did the future hold? More lands? Animals? People or even a big bed for her and Hatter to play in as part of, ahem, royal duties. Then again there was always the chance for children in her life in which Alice suspected that with Hatter being the last of the Hightops, he'd want a big family and given how much sex they seemed to get involved with that was quite a likely possibility. How many kids though? Three, Ten, Thirteen...maybe even fifty? Not q uite out the realms of possibility it must be said.

"Bloody hell I'm wet again," Alice muttered as that last thought made her moist even more. Regardless of whatever this curious girl was going to end up doing next, one thing was for certain. Truly, Alice was home in Wonderland.

AUTHOR NOTE

Thank you for reading this story, I hope you enjoyed it as much as i did writing it for you. The concluding part of the story will be in the next edition of this book attached to it as a series, hopefully, it would have been released by the time you are reading this. I will really love your feedback so i will have my eyes on my email inbox, so, therefore, please kindly use the comment section of where you purchased this book from to place your reviews, suggestion and ratings for this book for it will help me improve the forth coming stories that are yet to be released. You can contact me the author via my email (viaoptimisticdaily@gmaildotcom).

Printed in Great Britain
by Amazon